Natural Born
FLUXUS

NATURAL BORN FLUXUS

Also by Cecil Touchon

Sell People Things They Don't Need
Is it Necessary to Say Something?
Happy Shopping
Important Documents of Post-Dogmatism
The All New and Improved Neoist Manifesto
The Hidden Sphere of Artistic Concerns
Fluxus Event Scores of Cecil Touchon
The Cut and Paste Poets – An Anthology of Collage Poetry
The Spam Poetry Game
Natural Born Fluxus

Additional Books from
Ontological Museum Publications

Massurrealism – Images, No Text - James Seefaher
A Room of Illusions - Alan King

See all our publications at: lulu.com/ontological

Natural Born FLUXUS

Edited by Cecil Touchon

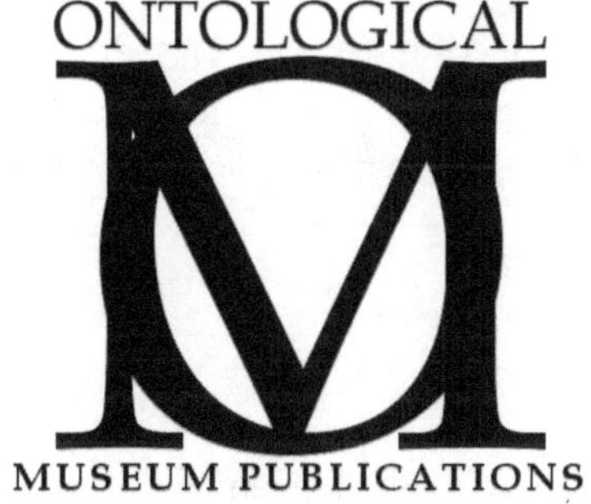

Ontological Museum Publications
Ontologicalmuseum.org

Cover Image: antique photo found at a Paris flea market from the permanent collection of the Ontological Museum

Cover Design: © 2008 by Cecil Touchon

The illustrations in this book are all images whose copyright use has been donated for use in this publication by the respective contributors

ISBN: 978-0-578-00333-7

Ontological Museum Publications
For contact information visit us online at:
Ontologicalmuseum.org

Printed in the United States of America.

Preface

The following are a series of event scores commemorating remembered small events from childhood that, in retrospect, share something in common with Fluxus activity. I first came up with the idea of scoring these events after corresponding with Ken Friedman related to his event score "Table Stack" which is dated from when he was about seven years old.

I was at first taken aback by the idea of designating childhood events as part of one's oeuvre but after a good deal of contemplation on the concept I came to realize that many events from childhood presage one's later life even though, as a child, we have no way to contextualize these events due to our lack of experience and control.

So it is possible then, later in life, with the skills and understanding in hand, to go back and dignify such events by recognizing their place in our artistic formation. By creating an event score for these experiences we integrate our childhood into our adult lives by viewing those experiences from an artistic point of view.

While we all have, by and large experienced the same events and thousands more in our own lives, what are telling are what specific events an artist chooses to select and all of the many others that are left to the side.

When writing these scores for my own book of Fluxus event scores, I decided that it would be a very interesting book project to invite my Fluxus colleagues that I know to participate with their own scores, childhood photos and other surviving documents.

I asked them to recalled their childhoods, identify those events that presage their future Fluxus activities and then commemorate those events with event scores and, if possible, send childhood photographs and other ephemera from their childhoods that fit the project. What we have ended up with is an endearing document of enduring value.

NATURAL BORN FLUXUS

Since the following scores are based on insight into remembered events, all are dated according to when the events first happened and also note the locations where the artists were when the events happened.

Cecil Touchon
Saturday, November 15, 2008

Acknowledgements

I would like to thank all of my Fluxus colleagues who took the time and care to contribute to the Natural Born Fluxus Project. I would also like to thank my wife Rosalia on whom I depend for helping to keep our lives together and on track as well as listen to the endless chain of ideas that bubble out of my mind continuously.

Dedication

In memory of George Brecht
August 27, 1926. - December 5, 2008

Introduction

Natural Born Fluxus is that tendency among artists to engage in Fluxus-like behaviors even if they never heard of Fluxus. Or possibly we could say that Fluxus ideas come out of a naturally occurring tendency in all artists that we now think of as Fluxus. It could be that the free wheeling nature of Fluxus allows artists to enjoy their creative, or at least peculiar, tendencies in an unfettered way that other forms of organized artistic activities do not.

Fluxus self consciously operates outside of the typical career oriented art world with its attention on credentials, collectablity, longevity and refined, complex technique development and instead focuses on the common everyday means available to literally anyone, anywhere.

The sorts of things that delight a Fluxus artist tend to be of an ephemeral nature, contain a humorous element and refer to that mysterious something that makes one laugh at a joke; call it irony or the unexpected twist, Fluxus artists enjoy a good surprise and a clever turn of phrase. They are willing to remain innocent enough to be easily amused and fall for a good trick.

It is this adherence to a child-like sense of wonder that this book hopes to illustrate.

Participants in this project represent the new vital community of Fluxus artists who are currently working together as a global community. This new group has emerged over the last ten years just as Fluxus was entering historical connonization. [i]
They are connected together via the internet creating group projects such as Fluxlist Box #1 - 1999; One Hot Minute, 2001; FLUXUATIONS CD from 2003, etc. They coordinate their efforts through several online email groups, blogs and web communities such as The Fluxnexus (fluxnexus.com), fluxusheidelberg.org, digitalsalon.com/weblog/, The Fluxlist, The Fluxlist Europe Blog and OpenFluxus.com.

NATURAL BORN FLUXUS

For the last year or two many of these artists have been starting to publish new Fluxus books. These include *Fluxus Vision* by Allan Revich, *Event Scores* by Walter Cianciusi, *Fluxus Flesh Power* by Litsa Spathi, *Fluxus Event Scores* by Cecil Touchon, *Ongoing Text by* Ross Priddle that also includes Cecil Touchon, Allan Revich, Ruud Janssen, Richard Rathwell, Andrew Riley Clark, Keith Buchholz, Litsa Spathi, Jukka-Pekka Kervinen, Reed Altemus, Roger Stevens and others, *Alan Bowman: Performance Texts 1998 – 2004* by Alan Bowman, etc. as well as this book; *Natural Born Fluxus.*

Contents

NATURAL BORN FLUXUS

1

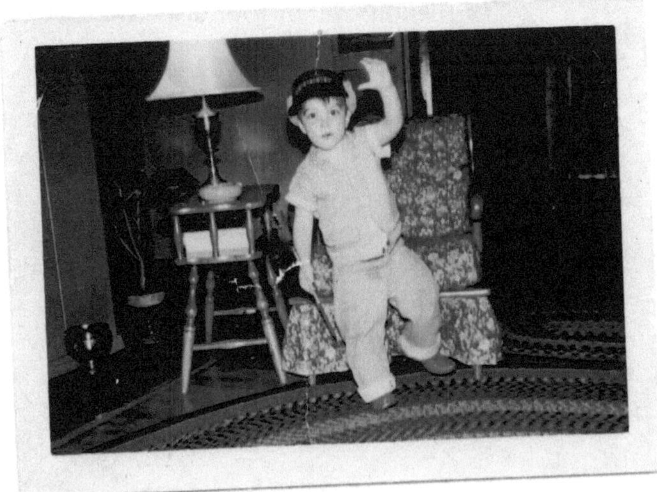

1958 – Fort Worth, Texas (at grandma's house)

Cecil Touchon

First Fluxus Event

Dirty Trick

Instruction: Shit in your diaper.

1956 - Austin, Texas

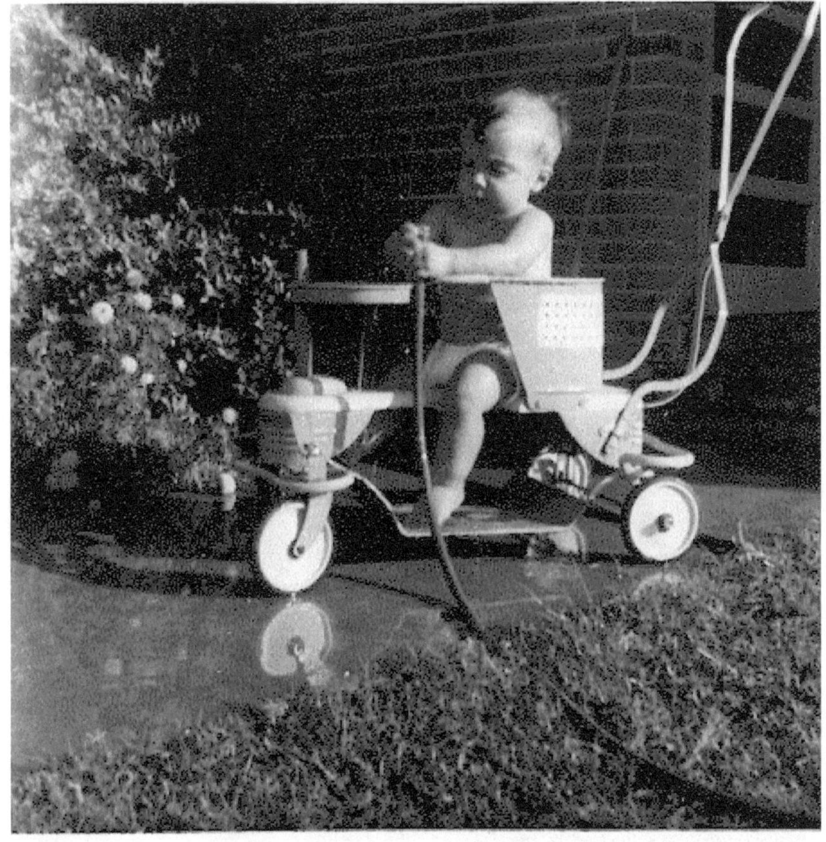

Playing with water 1956 – Austin, Texas

Event #2

Stack Blocks

Instruction: Stack blocks.

1958 - Fort Worth, Texas

Event #3

Sand Box Event

Instruction:

- Sit in a sandbox
- Put sand in your hair
- Dig sand out of your hair with finger-nails

1961 – Saint Louis, Missouri

Event #4

First 3-D Event: Draw a Cube

- Learn to imagine a 3D object in a 2D environment
- Draw a cube

1962 – Saint Louis, Missouri

Event #5

Pencil Music

Instruction

- Prior to class arrange to have classmates all push their pencils off the desk and onto the floor at the same time during class.
- At appointed moment participants drop pencils.
- Pretend it was a coincidence.

1965 – Saint Louis, Missouri

Event #6

Bomb a City Game

Instruction

Items: sheet of paper, pencil, needle

- Draw squares representing targets on a sheet of paper to look like a city.
- Turn sheet over
- Pretend you are dropping bombs by punching holes in the sheet with the needle
- Turn paper over and draw circles around pin holes to suggest range of damage.
- Inspect the imagined damage inflicted.
- Consider the cruelty of such an act.

1966 – Saint Louis, Missouri

Event #7

Build a House of Cards

Instruction

Items: deck of playing cards

- Construct a multi-level structure using all of the cards in the deck.
- Consider its fragility

1967 – Saint Louis, Missouri

Event #8

Fan Music

Instruction

- Listen to the sounds of a noisy fan till you fall asleep.

1968 - Saint Louis, Missouri

Event #9

The Daily Dilemma

Instruction:

Choose only one:

- Fudge Bar
- Eskimo Pie
- Dreamcycle

1968 – Saint Louis, Missouri

Event #10

Bury Performance

Instruction:
Bury something (or someone)

1969– Saint Louis, Missouri

NATURAL BORN FLUXUS

NATURAL BORN FLUXUS

2

Neil Horsky

Flying Elephant Event

Throw a stuffed elephant over a roof, back and forth with a friend.

Arlington, VA, 1988

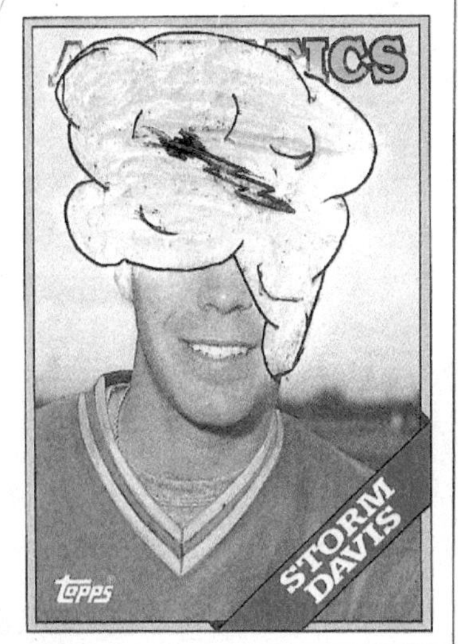

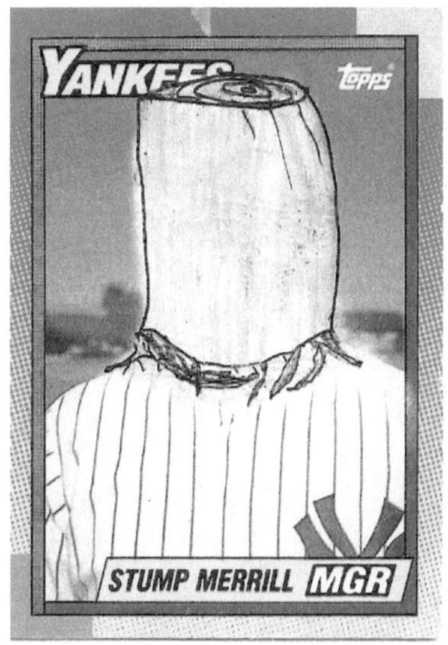

Artifacts from Baseball Card Event

Baseball Cards Event

Alter baseball cards to illustrate puns with the player's names.

Arlington, VA, 1991

Flashlight

Trap fireflies in a jar. Watch them blinking. Let them go.

Arlington, VA, 1986

Flux Science

Illustrate imaginary hybridized animal species.

Acton, MA, 1988

Fort Event

A pillow and sheet fort (with ottomans, loveseats, etc…)

Acton, MA, 1990

Logo Event

Create logos for fictional sports teams in obscure cities.

Acton, MA, 1991

Vestibule Music

Vestibule music: percussive sounds of a train on tracks heard through the latch in a vestibule,

France, 1997

Balancing Act

Balance fallen sticks and twigs in the boughs of a tree.

Littleton, MA, 1994

Water Racing Event

Race sticks and/or leaves down a brook (preferably with one or more falls, and two or more competitors).

Acton, MA, 1994

NATURAL BORN FLUXUS

3

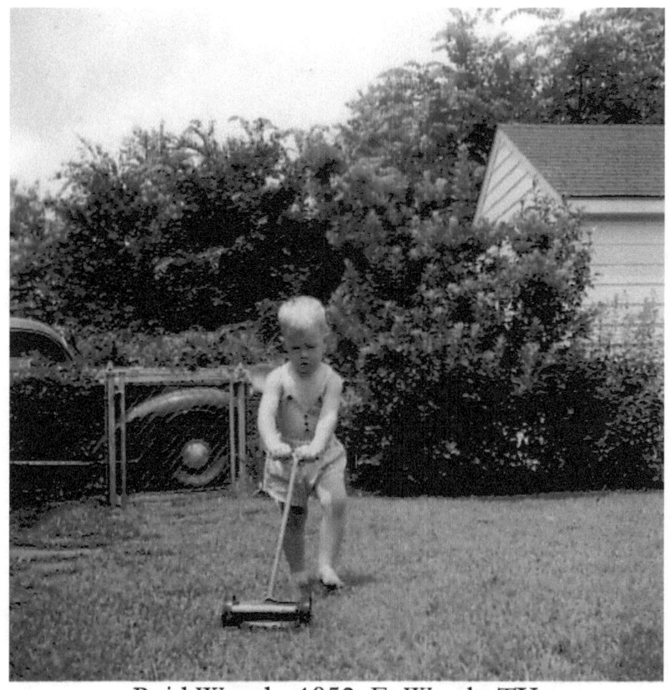

Reid Wood - 1952, Ft Worth, TX

Reid Wood

Event 1

Mow Grass

1952, Ft Worth, TX

Event 2

Eat Paint

a. Leave nursery school classroom.
b. Go to storage cupboard.
c. Open jars of paint.
d. Eat

1952, Chattanooga, TN

Event 3

Get Stamps

a. Go to father's desk.
b. Take postage stamps from roll in desk.
c. Glue postage stamps to inside of bedroom closet door.
d. Repeat.

1952, Chattanooga, TN

NATURAL BORN FLUXUS

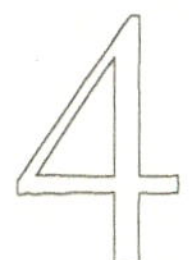

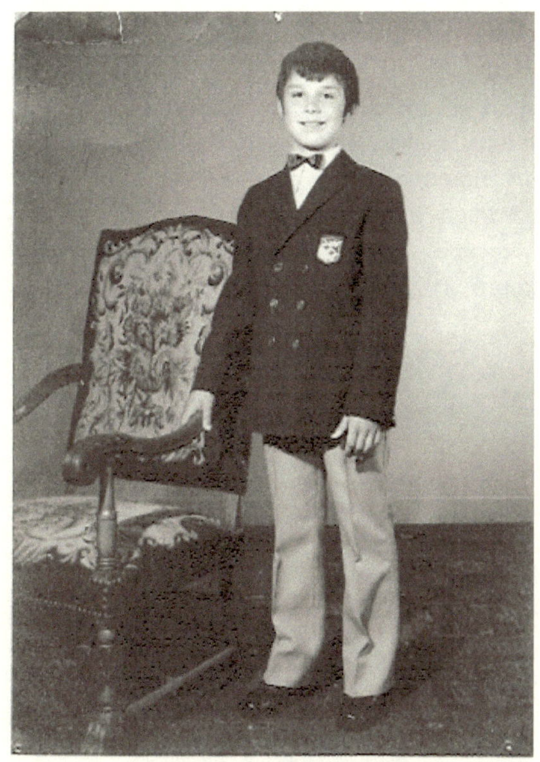

Mechelen(B) in 1973

Luc Fierens

Chair

Watch the chair
Take the chair
Sit in the chair
Tell a story of your childhood or a fairy-tale
once upon a time...
Look at the audience
Thank the audience by saying "dada"

Weerde (Belgium) 1973

Drawing Event (several performers)

a. take a piece of paper and draw a mirror
b. pass it on to someone and ask to draw something in the mirror (circle)
c. pass it on to someone else and ask to describe the drawing
d. show to the public

Weerde(Belgium) 1977

Whisper Event (more then 1 performer)

a. person A writes down a sentence
b. person A whispers a sentence in someone's ear (person B)
c. person B whispers this sentence in someone's ear (person C)
d. person C whispers this sentence in neigbor's ear (person D)
e. etc
f. last person shouts aloud the whispered sentence
g. person A shows the original sentence

Weerde(Belgium) 1973

NATURAL BORN FLUXUS

5

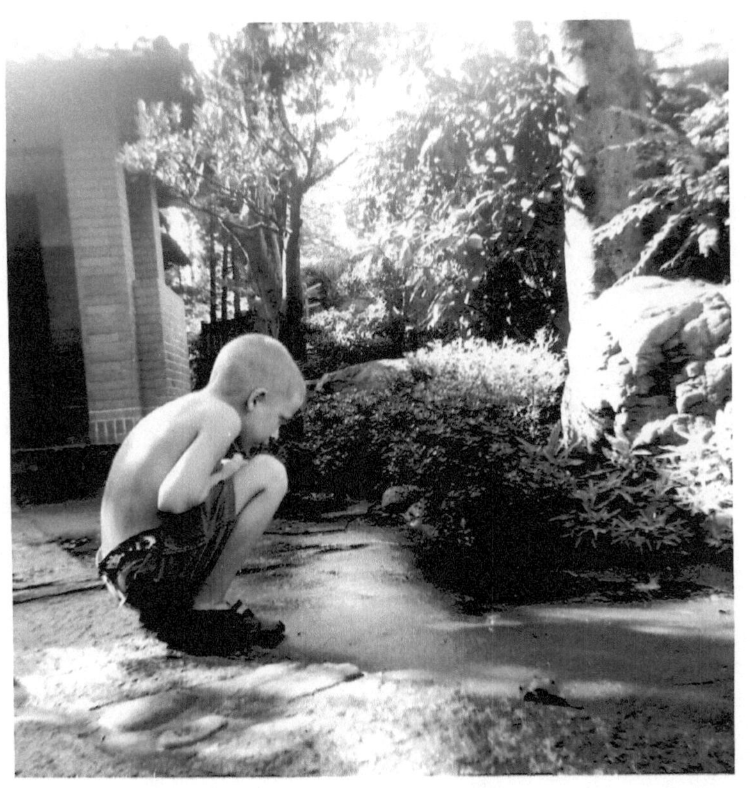

Japan, probably 1949

John M. Bennett

Wet Words

Book passage on a ship across the ocean. When out of sight of land, write a poem, fold and wrap it in transparent tape, and throw it into the waves. Repeat this every day until land again appears.

Pacific Ocean, 1948

Truck

Stand in a park and repeat the word "Truck" until it becomes completely meaningless and you can no longer pronounce it.

Columbus, Ohio, early 1940's

Bottle

Stand next to a river and repeat the word "Bottle" until it becomes completely meaningless and you can no longer pronounce it.

Columbus, Ohio, early 1940's

Postman

Sit in a car and repeat the word "Postman" until it becomes completely meaningless and you can no longer pronounce it.

Columbus, Ohio, early 1940's

Mist

Stand next to a washing machine and repeat the word "Mist" until it becomes completely meaningless and you can no longer pronounce it.

Columbus, Ohio, early 1940's

Pray to the Sun

Light the end of a piece of rope until it smolders and pray to the sun that it won't rain tomorrow.

Columbus, Ohio, ca. 1957

NATURAL BORN FLUXUS

NATURAL BORN FLUXUS

6

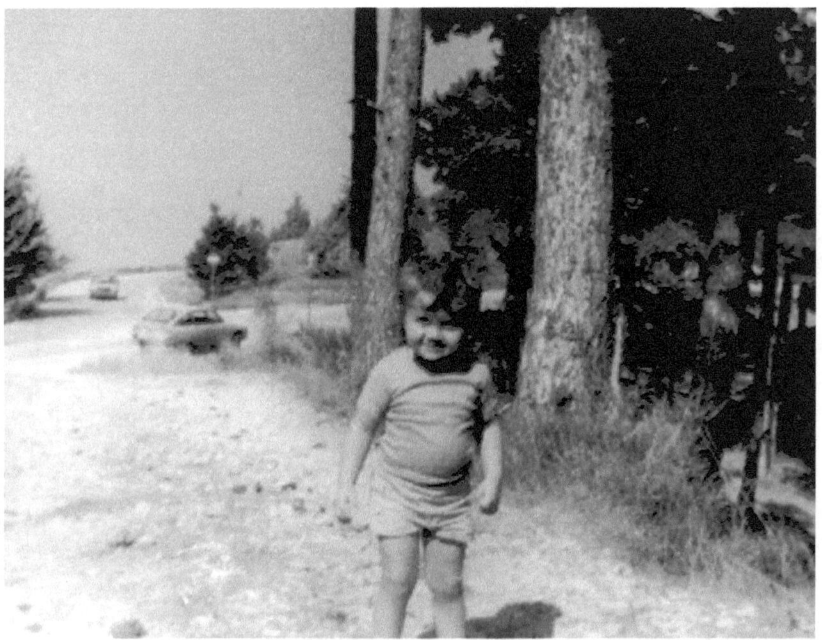

Mount Salviano, Avezzano, Italy
Trippaldello (Pot-Belly)

Walter Cianciusi

Drill Event

Drill a hole inside a woodblock each time you visit your grandfather.
Repeat until there's no more space to pierce.

1980

Accumulatore Zero

Pile Up all your 45rpm records on a player.
After 10 years pretend to be the inventor of the CD changer.

1982

NATURAL BORN FLUXUS

NATURAL BORN FLUXUS

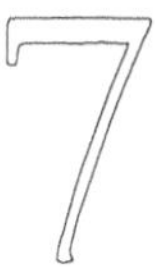

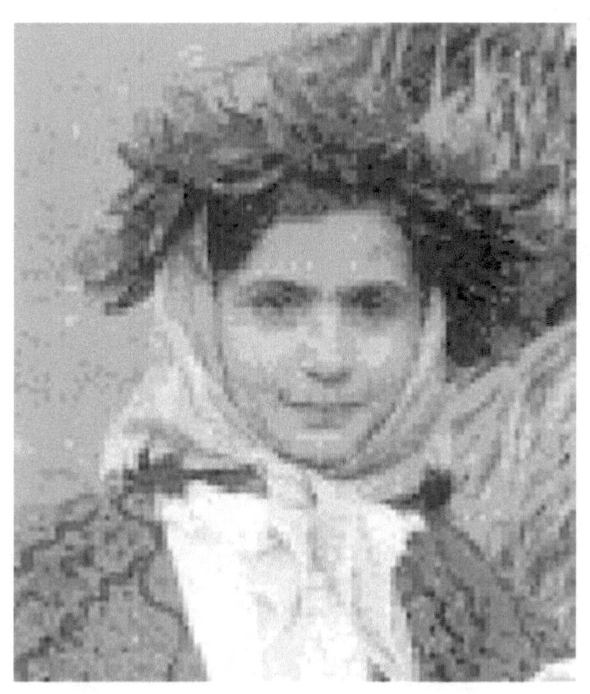

Litsa Spathi

Imaginary Flight Event

1. Get invited to do a performance with a publicum (a photographer)
2. Hear him speak the promise of: "a bird will fly out of the camera"
3. Concentrate on seeing the bird fly away
4. Wake up after you hear a click.

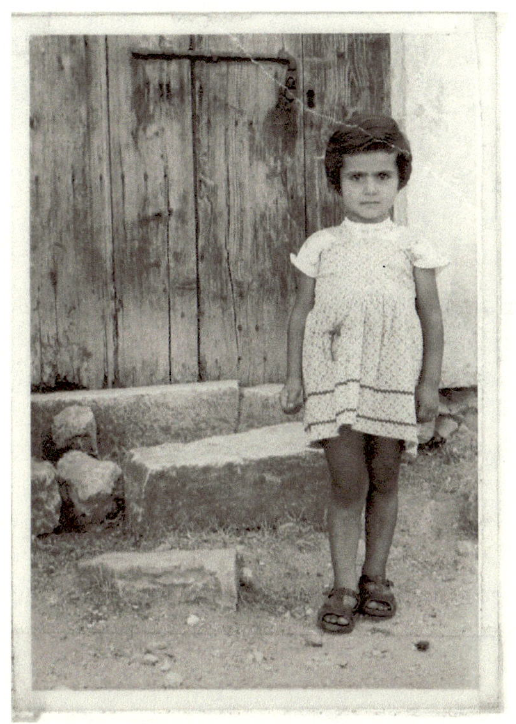

Litsa Spathi (1961 – 3 years old)

Organize a Coup Event

1. Organize a coup in your country
2. Wait one year.
3. Celebrate this jubileum with a theatre performance in your school.
4. Play the role of mother Earth.
5. Send your children into the war.
6. When played right, you get a crown made out of leaves to wear
7. Arrange a formal photograph to document the ending.

NATURAL BORN FLUXUS

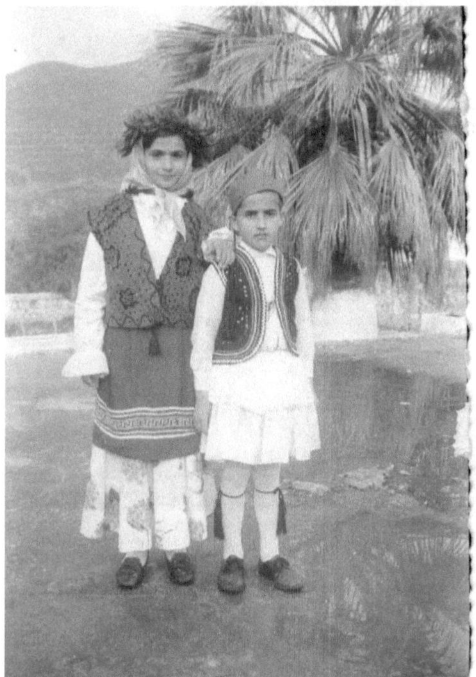

Litsa Spathi (1966 – 8 years old)
One year after the military coup in Greece.

NATURAL BORN FLUXUS

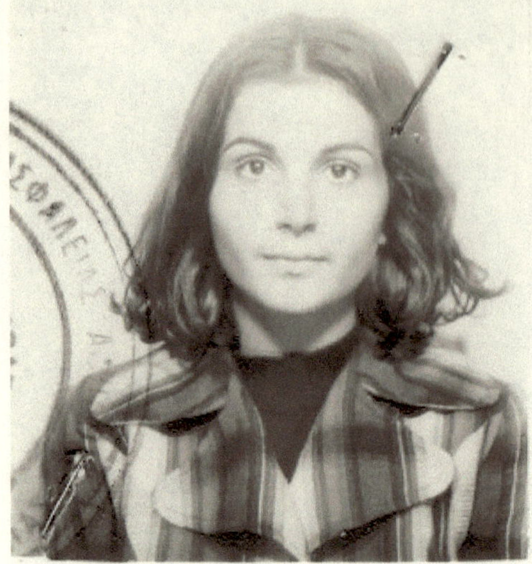

Litsa Spathi (1973 – 15 years old)

Leaving Event

1. Live under dictatorship without your parents.
2. Request for a passport to make it possible to leave the country.
3. Leave the country.

NATURAL BORN FLUXUS

ΥΠΟΔΙΕΥΘΥΝΣΙΣ ΓΕΝ. ΑΣΦΑΛΕΙΑΣ
ΚΣΤ' ΠΑΡΑΡΤΗΜΑ

ΒΕΒΑΙΩΣΙΣ

«Περί προσωρινής ... έκδοσιν δελτίου ταυτότητος»

ΕΠΩΝΥΜΟΝ (Μ[illegible] κεφαλαία) ΣΠΑΘΗ

ΟΝΟΜΑ [illegible]

» ΠΑΤΡΟΣ Νικόλαος

» ΜΗΤΡΟΣ Αικατερίνη

» ΣΥΖΥΓΟΥ ...

ΤΟ ΓΕΝΟΣ (έγγάμου γυναικός) ...

ΧΡΟΝΟΛ. ΓΕΝΝΗΣΕΩΣ 13-6-1958

ΤΟΠΟΣ ΓΕΝΝΗΣΕΩΣ [illegible]

» ΚΑΤΟΙΚΙΑΣ Αθήναι

Δ/ΝΣΙΣ ΚΑΤΟΙΚΙΑΣ οδός [illegible] αριθμός [illegible]97

ΕΠΑΓΓΕΛΜΑ ...

ΙΔΙΟΤΗΣ (Μαθητής, Στρατιώτης, Σύζυγος κ.λ.π.) μαθήτρια

ΔΗΜΟΤΗΣ [illegible] Αριθμός Δημοτ. 1647

ΜΗΤΡ. ΑΡΡΕΝΩΝ ... Αριθμός ...

ΘΡΗΣΚΕΥΜΑ Χριστιανή Ορθόδοξη

Ό αιτών ... την έκδοσιν του ύπ' αριθ. I145839/73 δελτίου ταυτότητος.

Ή παρούσα ... δελτίου ταυτότητος, ισχύει επί δύο μήνας από σήμερον και παραδίδεται επί τη παραλαβή του Δελτίου Ταυτότητος.

... τη 21/10/1973

... ΔΙΟΙΚΗΤΗΣ

ΙΩΑΝΝΗΣ Ε. ΑΝΤΩΝΟΠΟΥΛΟΣ
ΥΠΑΣΤΥΝΟΜΟΣ Α'

NATURAL BORN FLUXUS

8

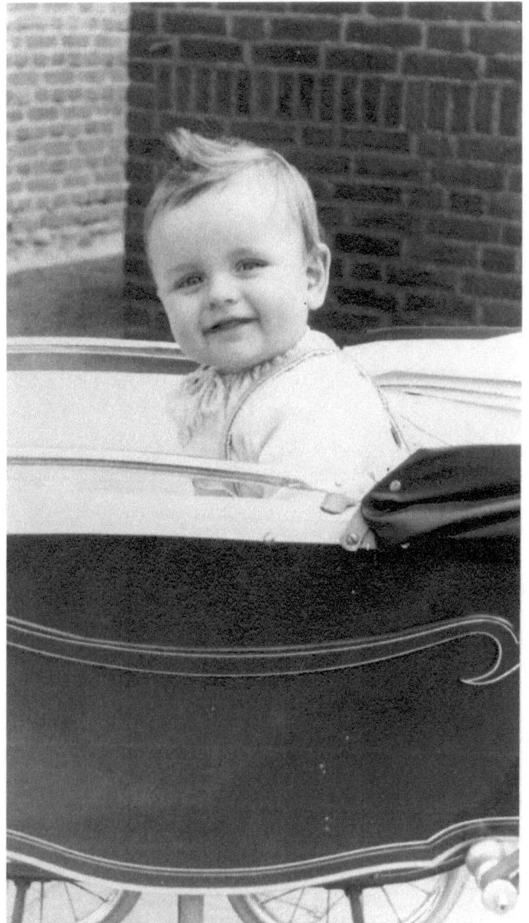

Ruud Janssen (1961 – 2 years old) Tilburg, Netherlands

Ruud Janssen

Smile Event

1. Ask your mother for the Bentley
2. Let her drive you through the street
3. Smile at everybody that you pass

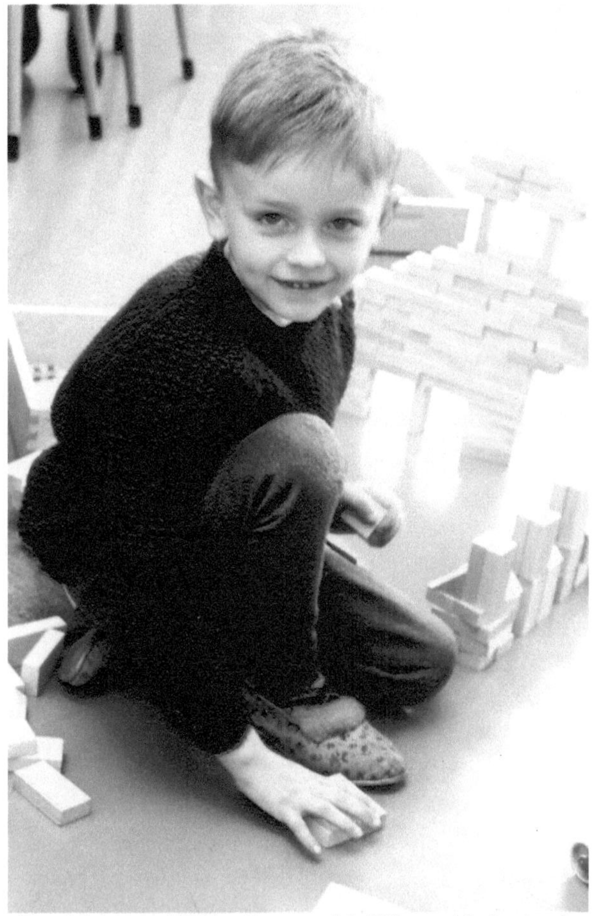

Ruud Janssen (1964 – 5 years old) Tilburg, Netherlands

Retire Event

1. Go to "Kindergarten"
2. Claim all the wooden Bricks that they have in the classroom
3. Build a church and a complete street.
4. Sell them to all other children
5. Retire

NATURAL BORN FLUXUS

NATURAL BORN FLUXUS

9

Brad Brace

NATURAL BORN FLUXUS

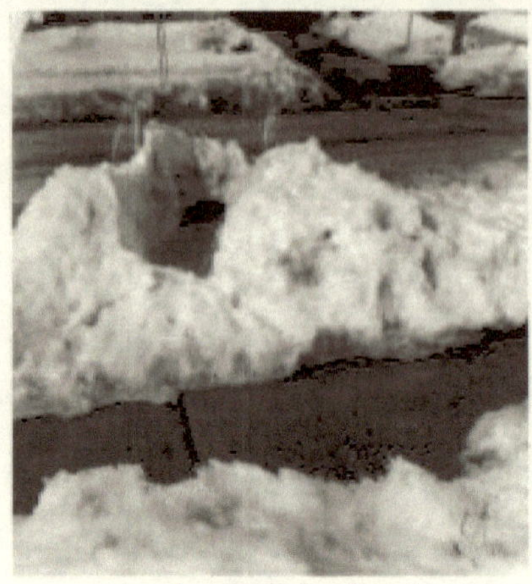

(my homemade photo)

Shovel Event

shovel the snow
into a big heap
then, dig that.

1961 - 7 years old

10

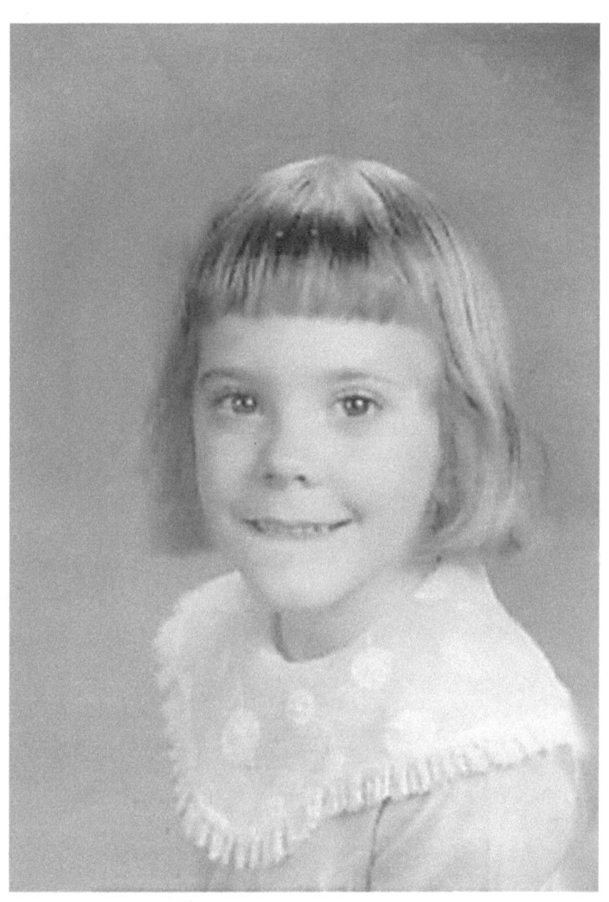

Sheila Murphy

Fencing: A Score in Seven Parts

1. Get sword.
2. Fight duel.
3. Assess own competence.
4. Order new sword.
5. *Discuss.*
6. Challenge others.
7. Continue quest for excellence.

circa 1962

September 29, 1962

Dear Dad,

I hope you have a lovely trip. I love you. Would you get me a sword (play) in Europe when you get me the other thing in Europe. Because I have been learning to fence. I beat Dick to a dual and one time I beat Mark. Mark took lessons for fencing and he has a book that tells all about fencing. He taught me the steps for fencing. And when you come back I will swordfight with you too. I love you.

Love
Sheila

Letter to Dad 1962

Treehouse Event

1. Look up the tree 9 feet.
2. Make platform comfortable.
3. Invite.
4. Think about the neighbor.
5. Enjoy the quiet.
6. Have another word for things.

Flute Event

1. Play the flute in the screened in porch.
2. Thank Bobby Best for mentioning that he likes to listen while he showers.
3. Thank Mother for saying that she likes to listen, period.
4. Play things by ear.
5. Invent new things.
6. Keep the springs from corroding.
7. Go to the flute factory in Elkhart and listen.

Listen & Tell Event

1. Listen to the Syburgs talk about interesting events.
2. Think about how interesting events can be.
3. Tell stories and try to improve the telling.
4. Listen to people.
5. Wish that it would never rain.

Demo/lition Event

1. Give a demo on how to use a record player.
2. Pull off the arm of the player by accident.
3. Try to fix it.
4. Keep the talk going.

11

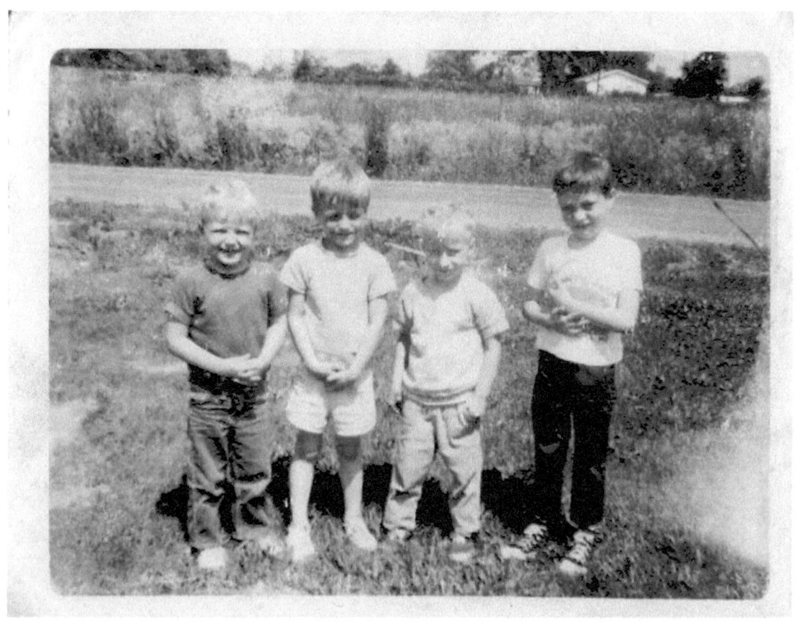

Keith Buchholz

Farm Event

Carry Chicken

Greenville, Illinois 1963

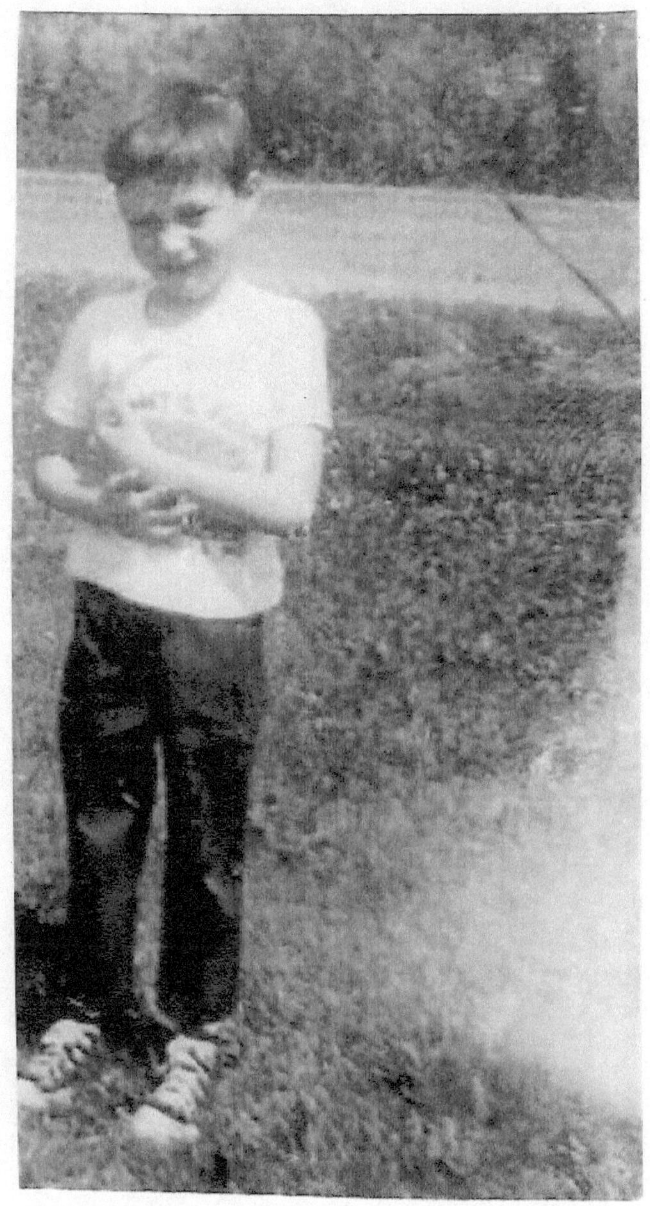

Photo Opportunity Event

Control the Image

Greenville, Illinois 1969

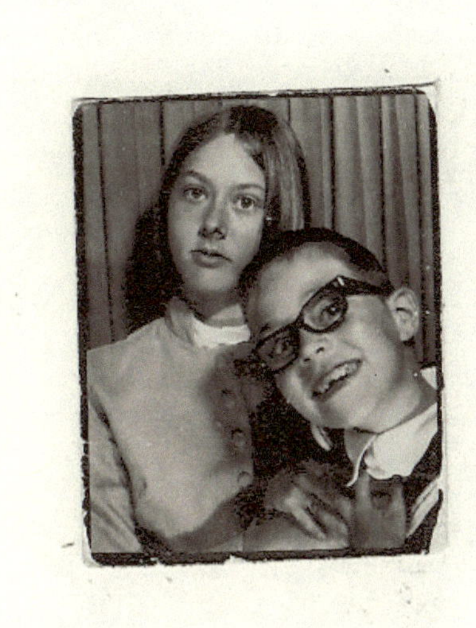

Spectacle Event

Look Sharp

Greenville, Illinois 1970

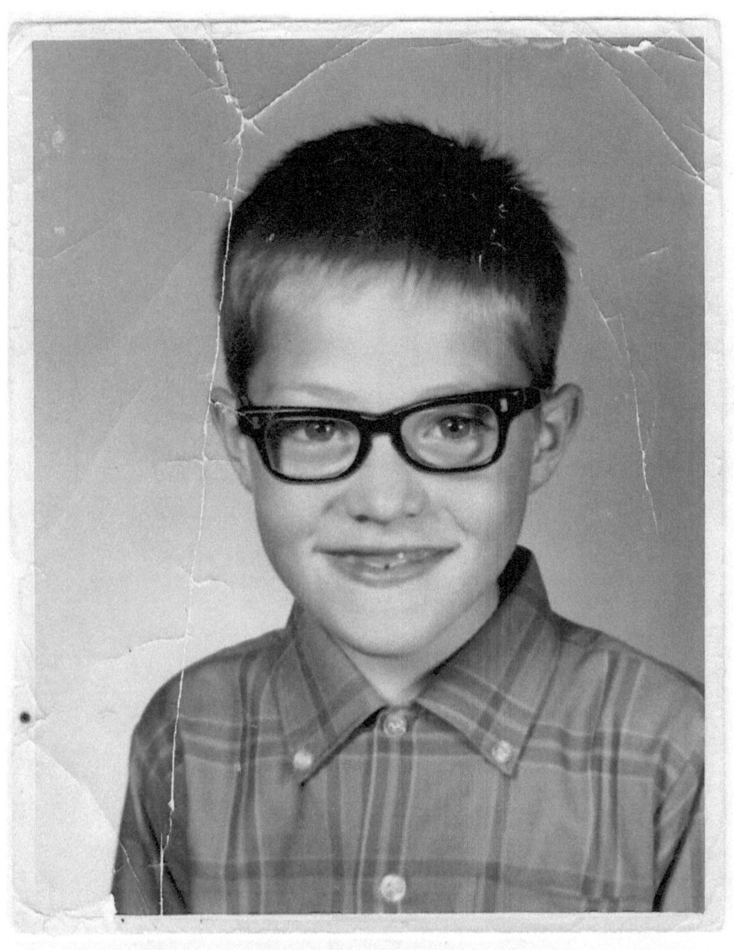

Political Event

Protest!

Greenville, Illinois 1963

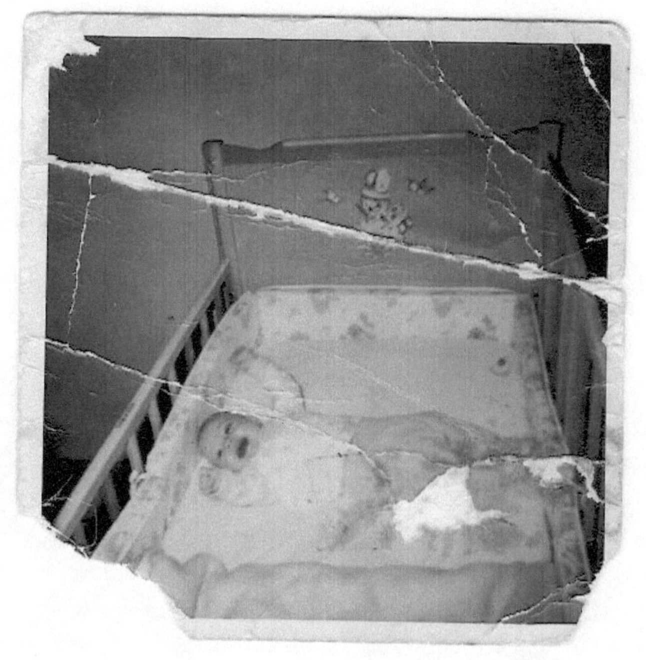

Signing Event

Sign Everything

Greenville, Illinois 1968

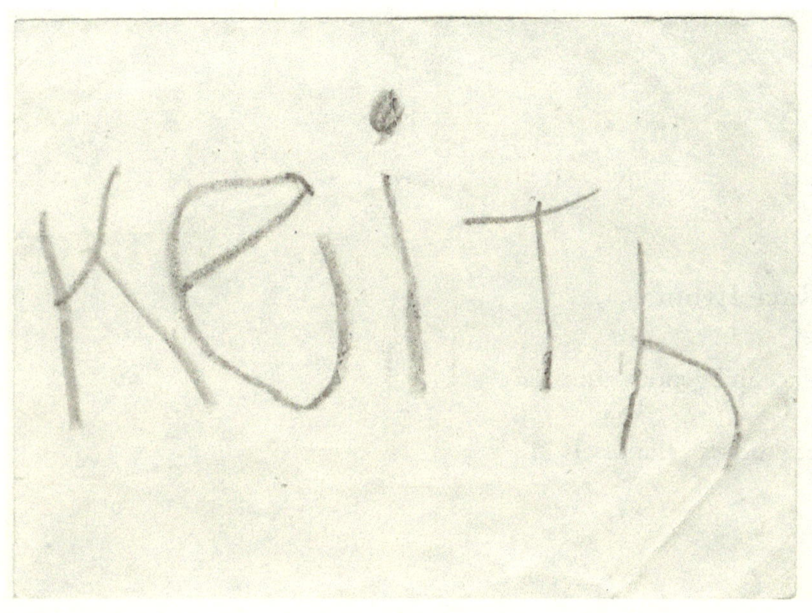
KeiTh

Race Event

Race indigenous animals

Smithboro, Illinois 1971

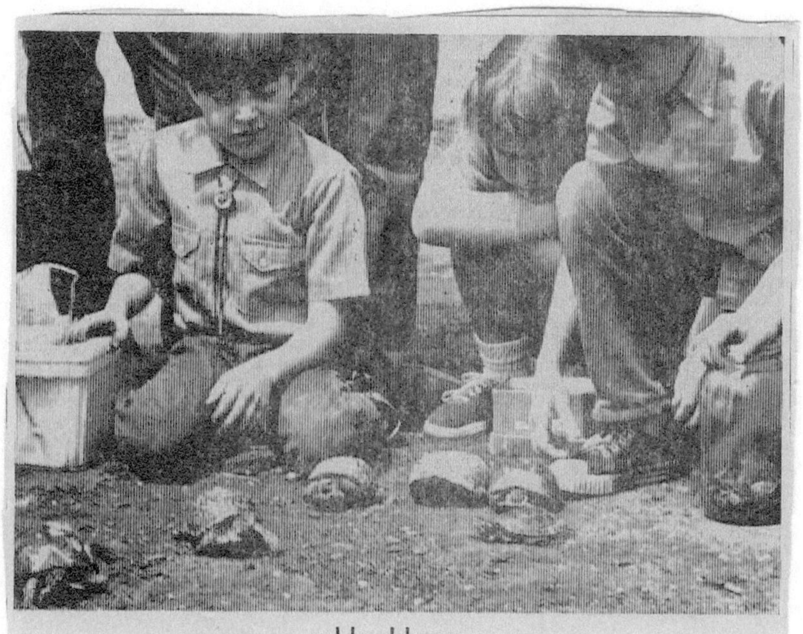

Ho Hum

Coffin Event

Contemplate mortality

Branson, Missouri 1975

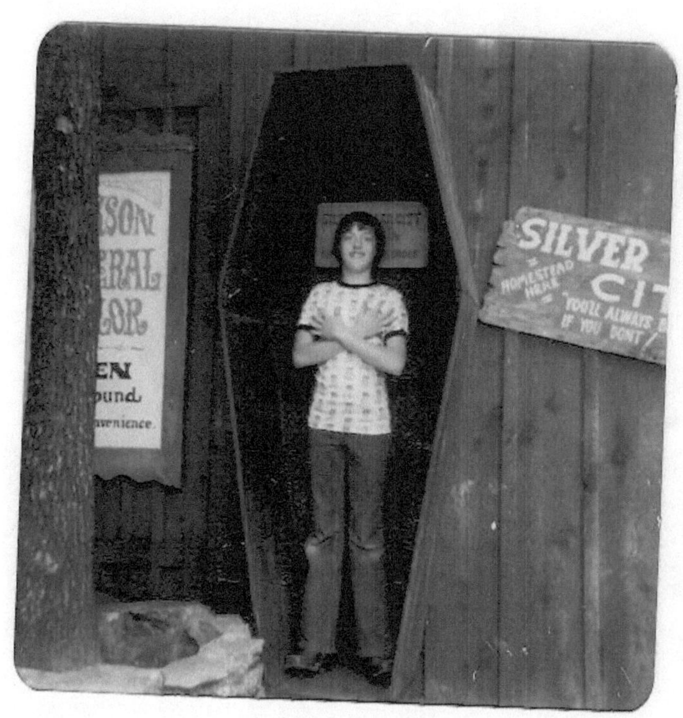
SILVER
HOMESTEAD HERE

Cowboy Event

Be a cowboy

Greenville, Illinois 1973

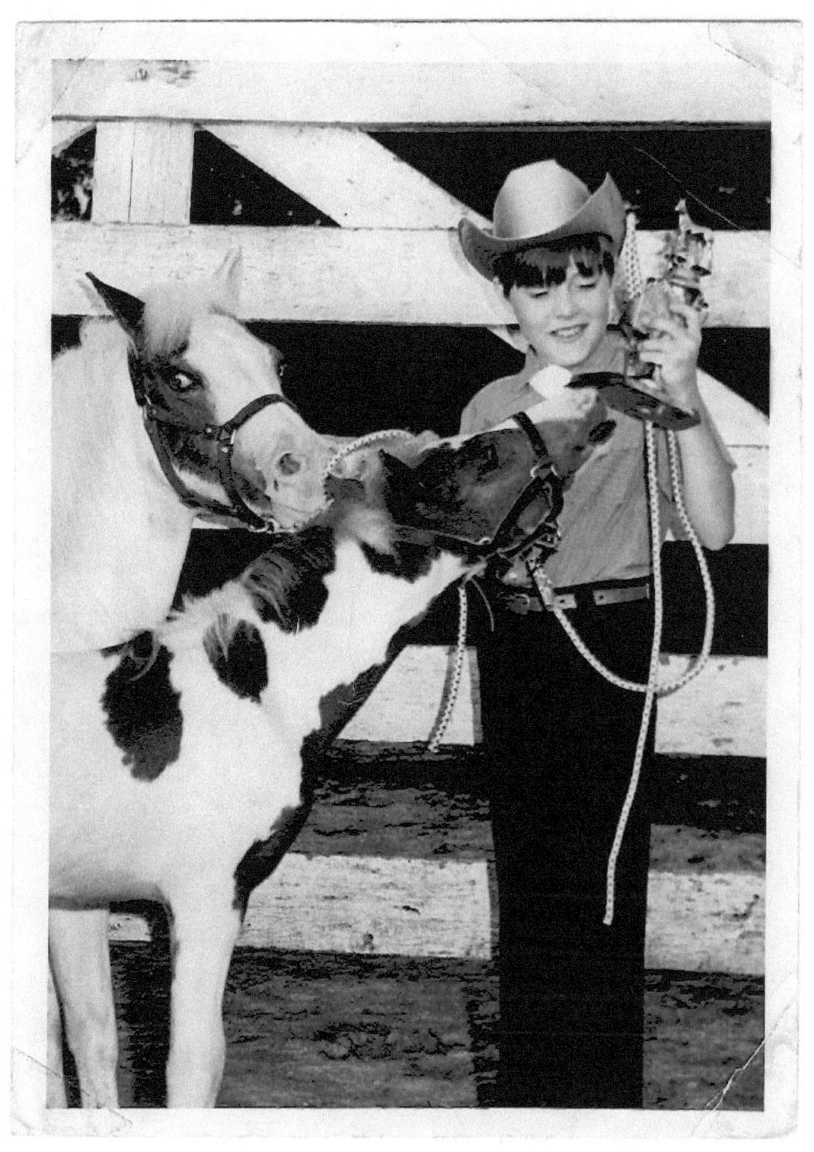

Association Event

Hang out with weirdos

Saint Louis, Missouri 1973

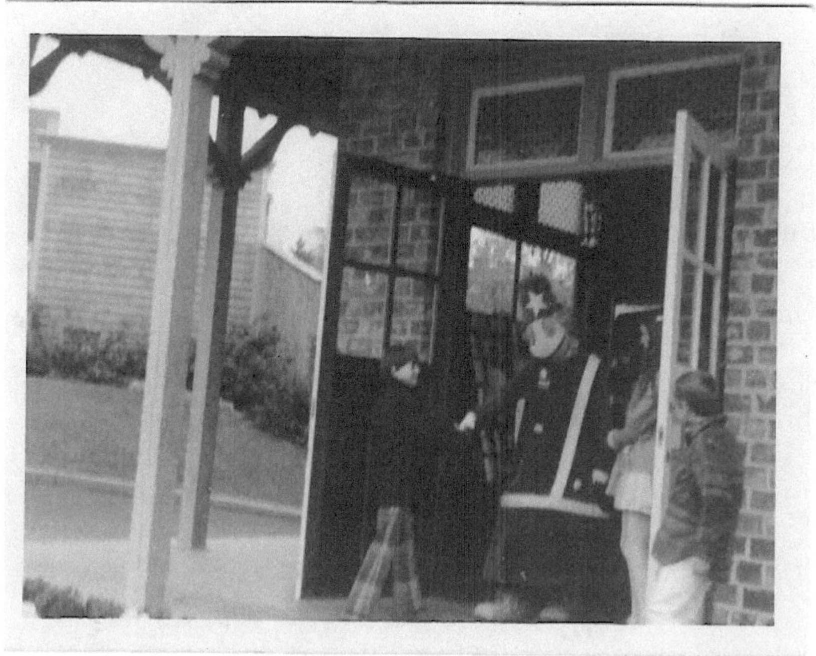

Build Event

Build! Build! Build!

Smithboro, Illinois 1971

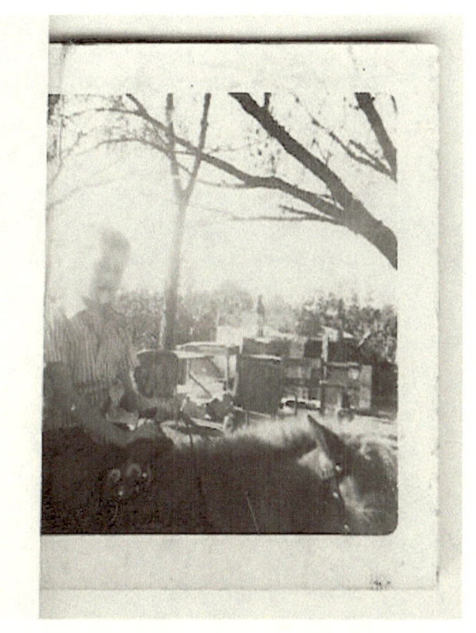

12

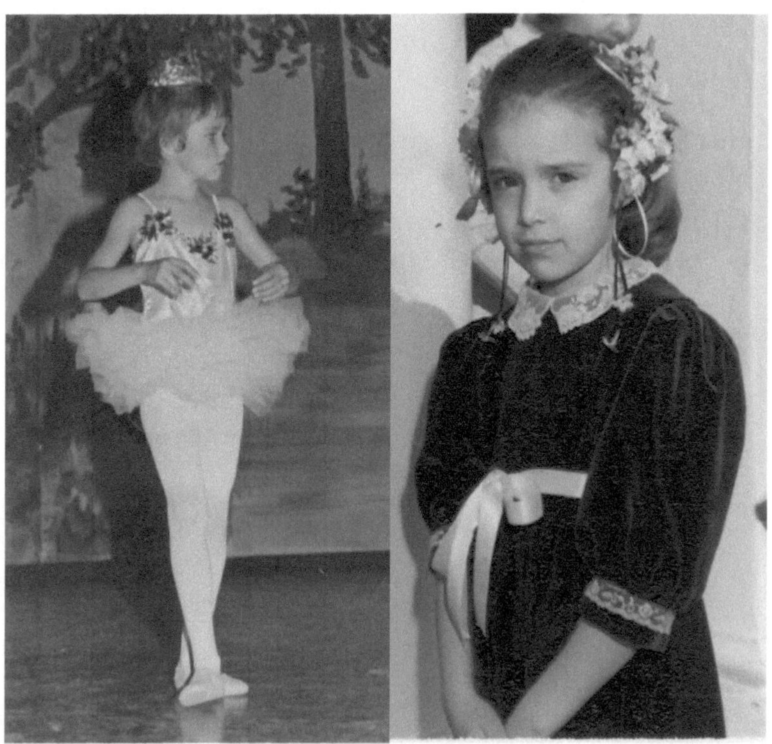

Two photos of Bibiana Padilla Maltos

Bibiana Padilla Maltos

Mouth clean

1. grab a bar of soap
2. bite right in the middle.
3. spit it out of shower

(Tijuana, Mexico 1975 – 1978)

Collections I

1. see "mouth clean"
2. collect the spat soap in a drawer

(Tijuana/Mexicali, Mexico 1975 – 1980)

Collections II

1. look for lizards in the palm trees
2. grab them by the tail
3. collect the tails in a shoe box

(Mexicali, Mexico 1984)

White Surprise

1. make sure parents are gone
2. take the buffer out
3. take the "turtle wax" out
4. wax the parquet floor with them
5. yell "surprise" when parents walk in

(Mexicali, Mexico 1982)

Sister Event

1. listen to your older sister
2. remind her you are sisters

(Tijuana, Mexico 1976-1978)

Funerary Event

1. attend a funeral service
2. ask your dad why people die
3. stand still, horrified
4. ask who will burry us if we all die at the same time

(Tijuana, Mexico 1977)

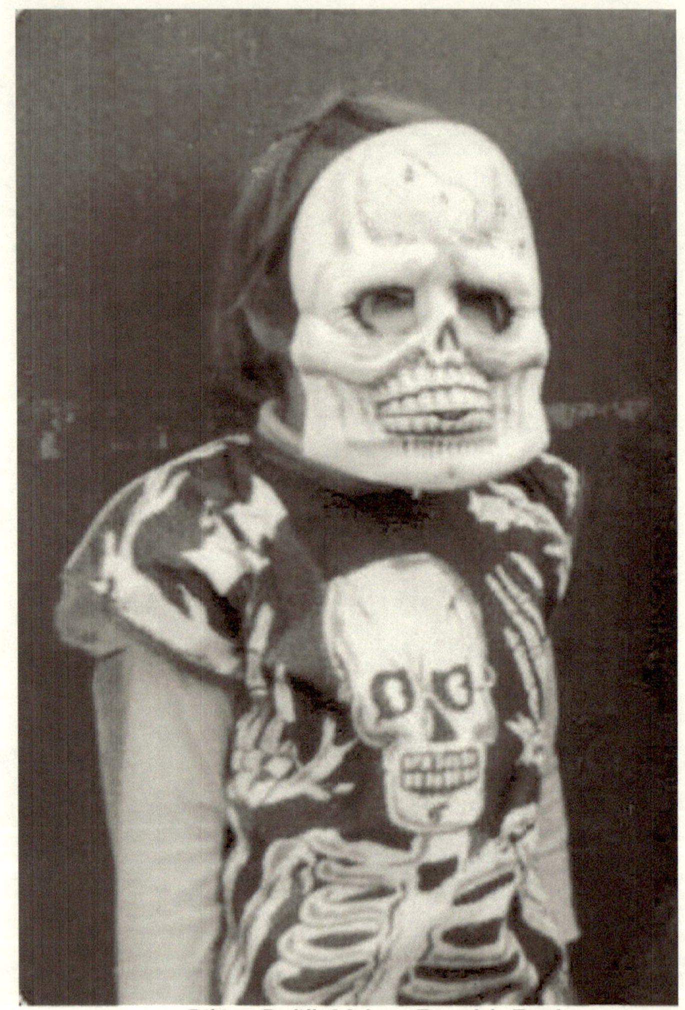

Bibiana Padilla Maltos – Day of the Dead

Copy Cat

1. ask your sister if you can pet the cat
2. adopt another cat because she doesn't want you to hold hers
3. name your cat the same name as your sister's cat

(Tijuana, Mexico 1977)

13

Gregory Steel

Score, "for Krupa"

1) Play a drum solo for as long as it takes to drive your parents out of the kitchen.

2) Raid the refrigerator and eat as much Birthday cake as possible before getting caught.

3) Claim you were driven into a trace by your drumming and ate the cake because the spirits told you to.

4) Return to playing the drums till the sugar high from the cake wears off.

5) Sleep

6) Repeat

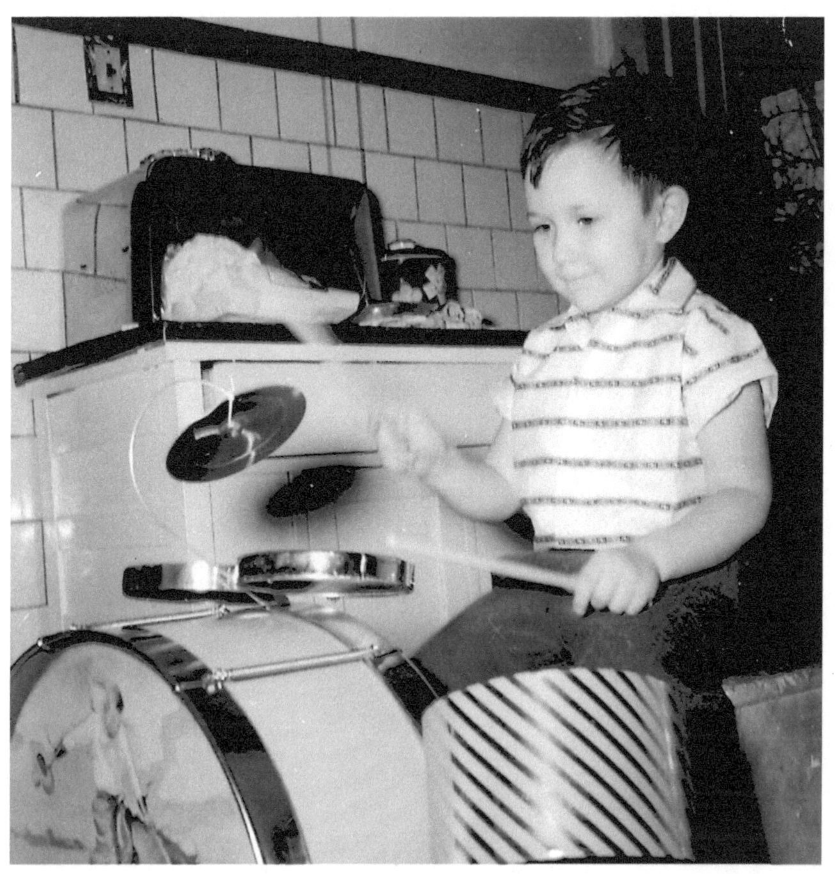

February 1957

score " Device"

1) point your device at the person taking your picture.

2) tell them that your device will not allow them to take your picture.

3) look serious and threatening.

4) refuse to look at the finished picture.

5) continue to believe in your own reality.

Easter 1956

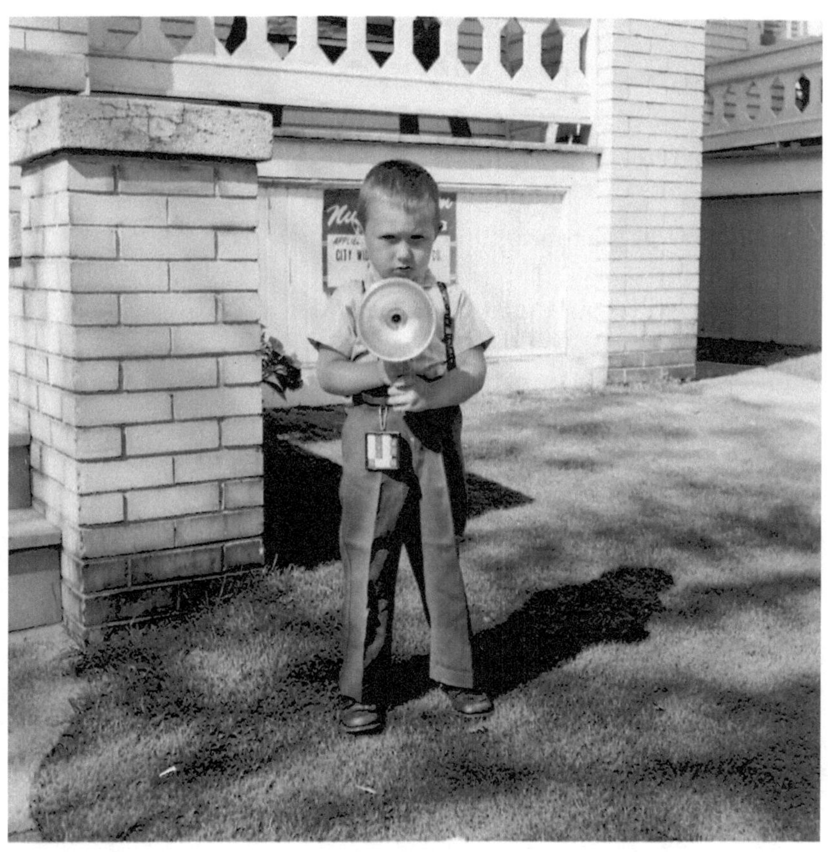

score, "Listen"

Gregory Steel, December, 1956

1) lay down with your ear to the carpet.

2) Listen to what the carpet is saying for ten minutes.

3) Tell someone else what the carpet said.

4) Play with your toys.

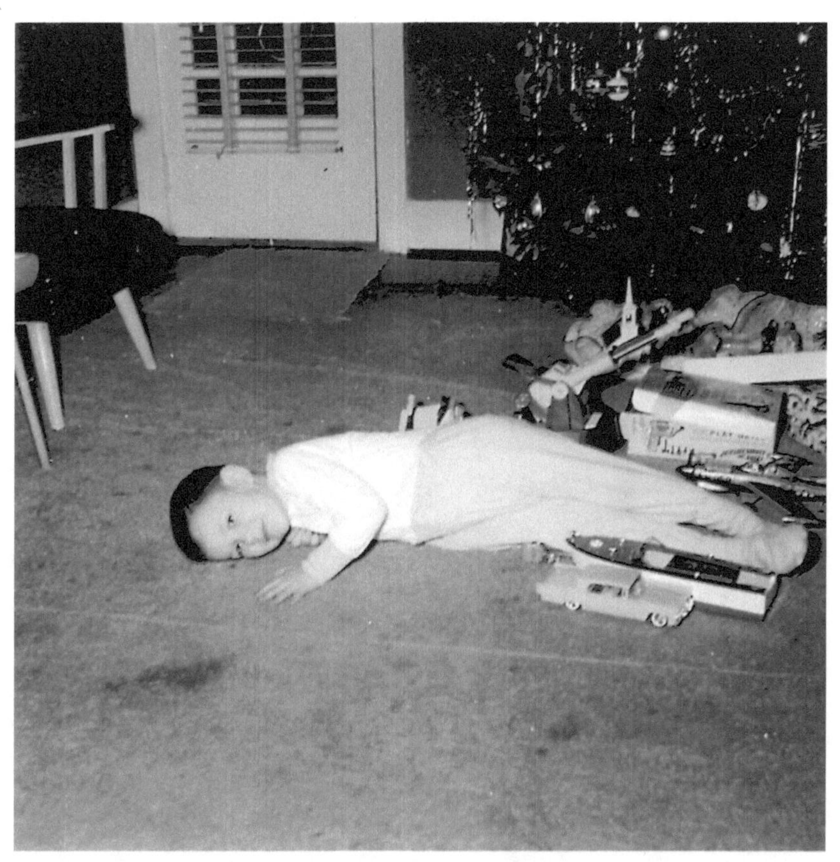

14

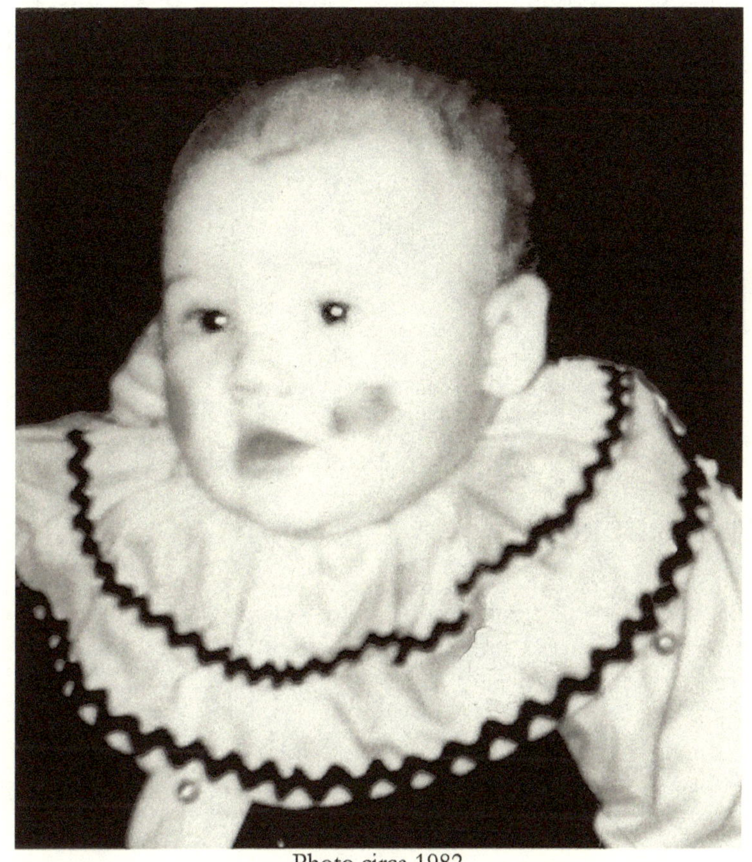

Photo circa 1982

Eric KM Clark

White Noise

My sister used to find me downstairs in my room gazing into a television that was only showing static. I used to also enjoy taking naps while having static play.

Sometime in the early 1990s
Victoria, BC

STATIC MIRROR

Find a channel on a television or a radio (or any current device) that only plays/shows static (white noise or similar).

Enjoy.

15

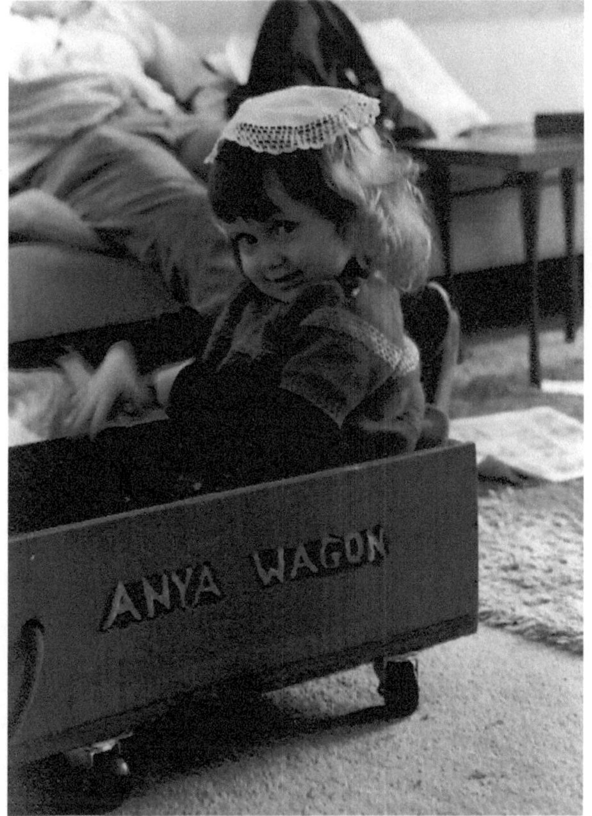

Riding around my grandparent's house in the "Anya Wagon" with an early ode to Dali's baguette on my head....a doillie I found under a plant in the living room."

Anya E.V. Liftig

Event 1

a. take a book (s) off a book shelf
b. organize book (s) in piles according to size and shape
c. create walls out of book piles
d. continue until all books have been removed from all shelves in house
e. inhabit book fort until adult replaces books back on shelves (usually many weeks later)

Westport, CT USA 1983

Event 2

a. find blue marker
b. find body part to be operated on
c. draw elaborate instructions for doctor re: operation.
d. proceed to operating room

New Haven, CT USA 1984

Event 3

a. find scissors
b. locate pigtails on your head
c. cut them off
d. find jar of peanut butter in kitchen
e. smear peanut butter all over hair and forehead
f. call pet dog
g. let dog lick off peanut butter

Westport, CT USA 1980

16

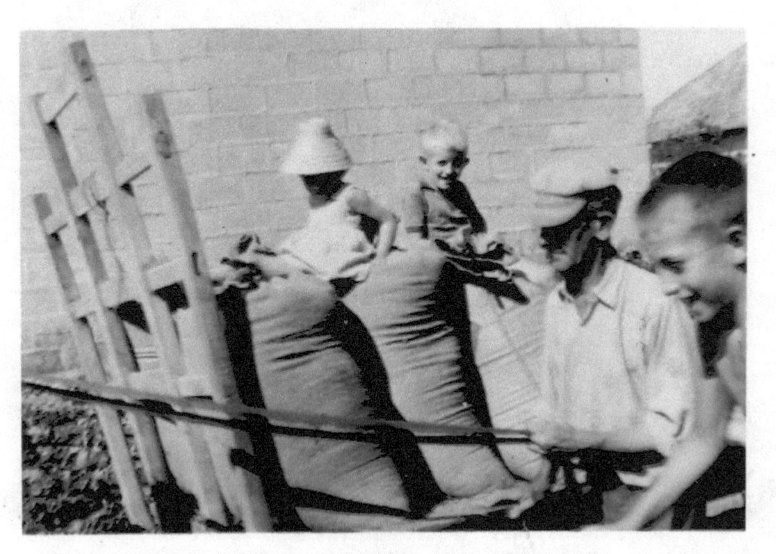

Yves Maraux

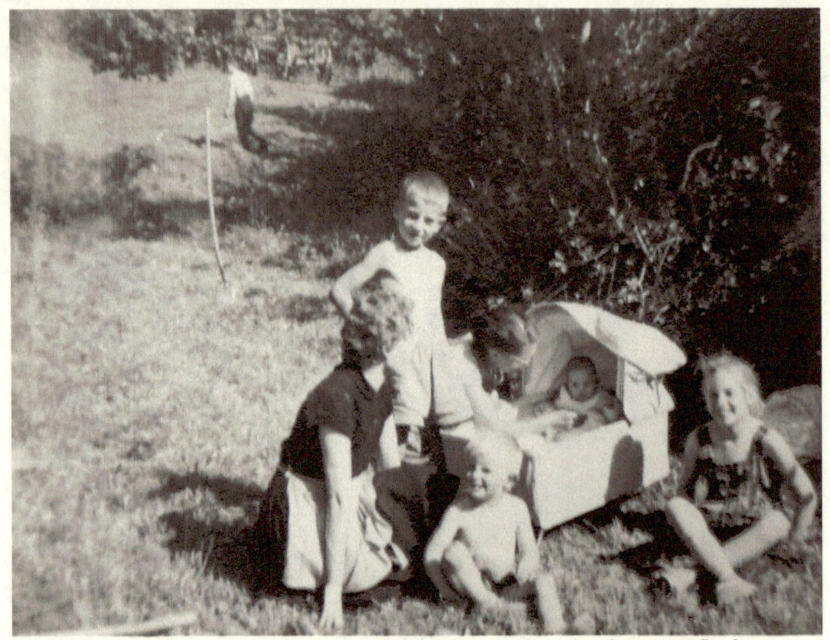

1958 at Saizenay 39 Fontaine Riche a meadow in the Jura fir forest France. I'm eating a blade of grass looking at the camera

<u>Thus far shall you go and no farther</u>

The Fairground Psychoanalyst Stall

Some tent for the psychoanalyst stall

(le cabinet d'analyste en baraque foraine)

A Mobile Divan like a Wheelbarrow

During buziness hours anybody can come and read some insulting letter for somebody he consider as an economic saboteur (dedicated to the local museum curator)

The Sound Mill

Ride a bicycle with iron wheels to make sound in crushed gravel.

appartement bicycle with own electric equipment so the use generates power for sound player with record of crushed gravels under iron wheel ... different speeds , light system is image projector (video , slides , sup8 etc computer etc) , landscaping crossing experience ....

home grown potatoes

Make a pile of plastic bags full of earth and some potatos.
Staple to the kitchen wall.
Water with some tea , coffee, etc

Four Scores for a Primal Workshop in Generative Phonology

(primal as pre articulate language)

Speech pattern is recited according to one's native tongue.

Performer stands further away from phonation apparatus (mike) as physical training in vocal exercises improve.

Pulsations to be formulated through alphabetical sounds .

score 1 / oralature

recorded bibble babbling audio clusters from (known) poets

score 2 / bibble babble postcards

Standard postcards with some chips that make sound when opening it, this sound is bibble babbling on display

score 3 / mother & child

Set up an event in a meeting room of nurslings and mothers with soft feed back sound system. let children bibble babble softly on the sound system

score 4 / apprentice nursling choral

Give the audience soft drinks, bibs and some requested instruction in natural and generative phonology (Schwitters ursonat could be used as intro if necessary) - superdada dress and conductor's baton for choral director

17

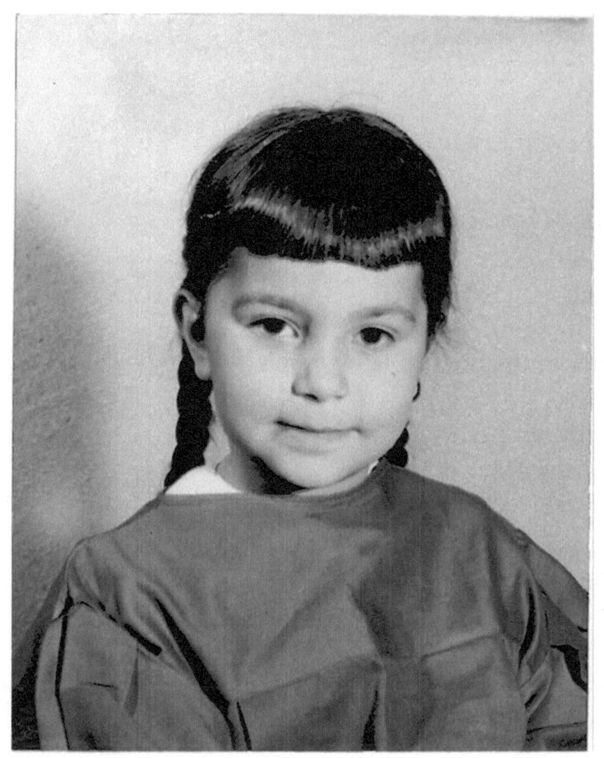

Christine Tarantino

Event/Memory #1 Bakery

1. 'Work' in family bakery store.

2. Rearrange breads displayed by shapes.

3. Rearrange cookies displayed by colors.

4. Encourage customers to buy items by shapes/colors.

Christine Tarantino
1954, Bronx, New York

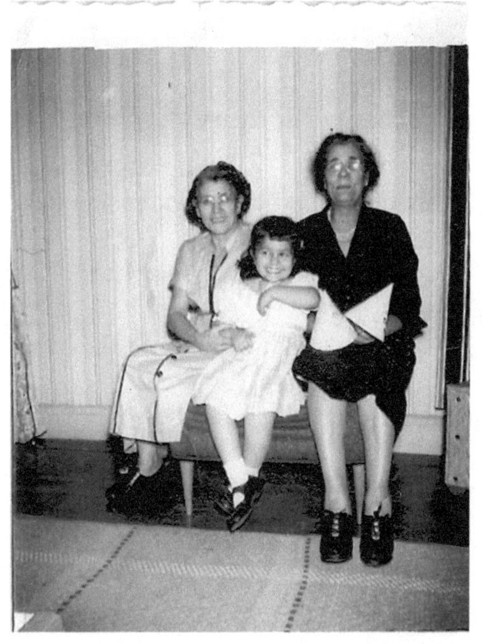

Event/Memory #2 Food

1. First day, eat only foods that begin with the letter "A".

2. Second day, eat only foods that begin with the letter "B".

3. Third day, eat only foods that begin with the letter "C".

4. Continue through the alphabet until boredom sets in.

Christine Tarantino
1958, Boston, Massachusetts

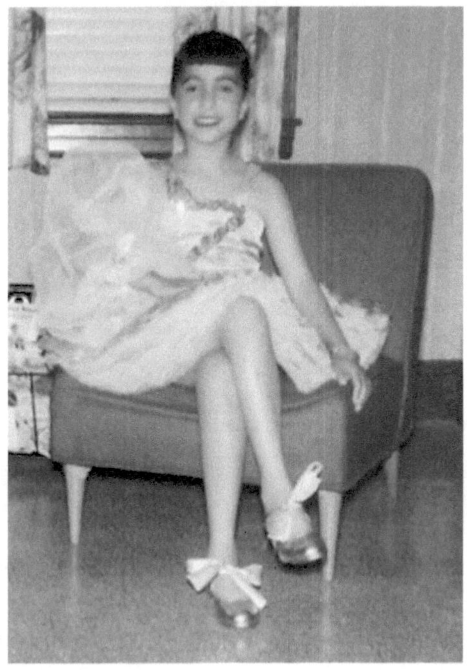

Event/Memory #3 Dictionary

1. Take the family dictionary off bookshelf.

2. Beginning with the "a" words cross out words I don't like with a black marker.

3. Cut apart map of USA in back of dictionary.

4. Rearrange states to form a new shaped country.

Christine Tarantino
1957, Boston, Massachusetts

Event/Memory #4 Contest

1. Enter a jingle for "Gillette" contest.

2. Lie about age on entry form.

3. Win the contest.

3. Become disqualified when parents receive prize notification.

Christine Tarantino
1960, Boston, Massachusetts

18

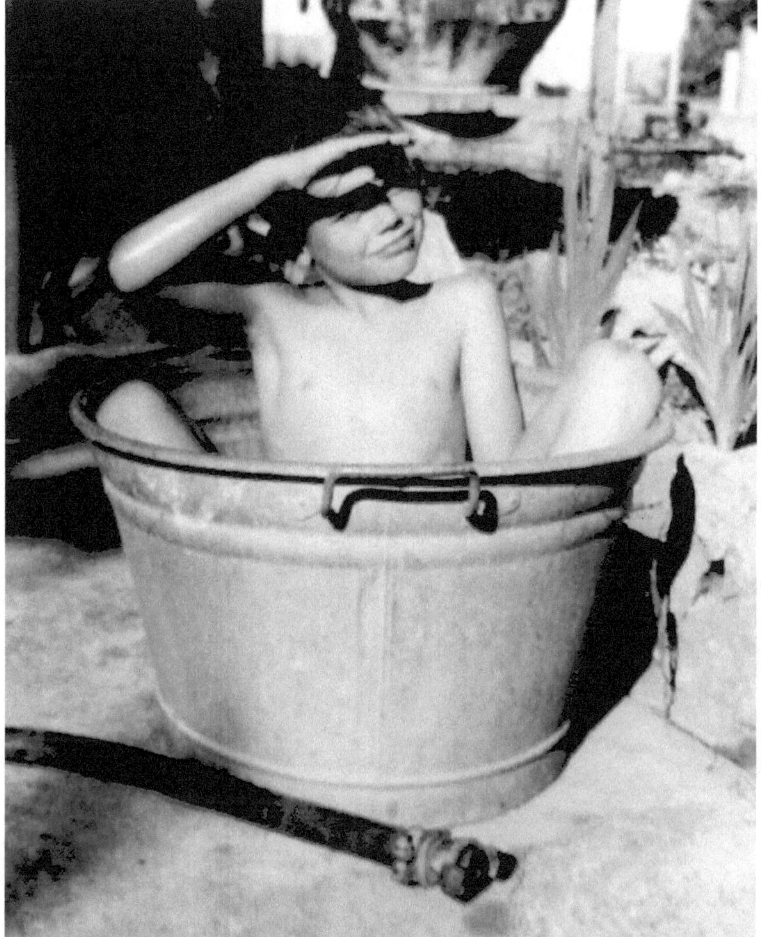

Born, at the moment alive ... sometimes washed in bathtubs ... sometimes getting in contact with the fluxus sun ... what will come next ?

Roland Halbritter

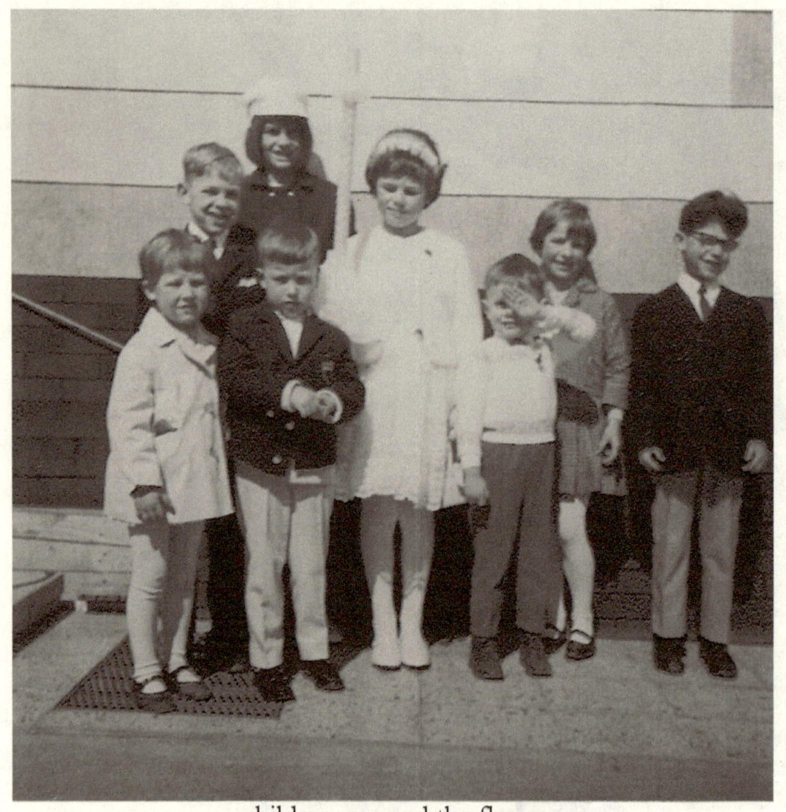

children, me and the fluxus sun

19

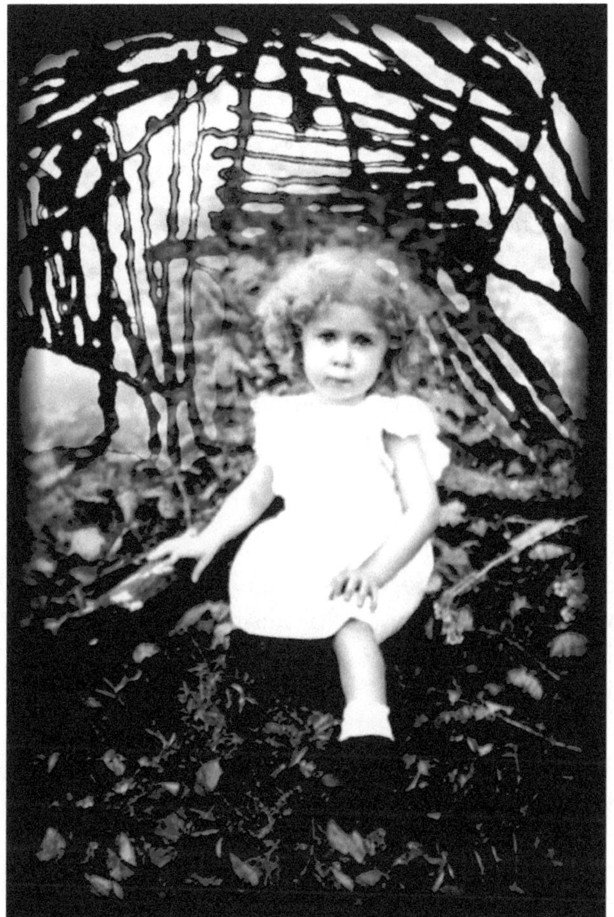

I See Sticks is Princess Lorraine (pre siblings) sitting beside the Rideau Canal in Ottawa, Canada (1946). The overhead structure is a transparency of a dome lamp (based on stick forts) that I made of twigs in the 1980s.

Lorraine Kwan

Score for Sticks

1. Build a fort in the woods with sibs
2. Go to kitchen cupboard, find one square of unsweetened chocolate, take to the fort, share
3. Go to the kitchen cupboard, find one box of jello, take to the fort, each take licks
4. Go to the kitchen cupboard, fine a bag of coconut, take to the fort, share
5. Go to the kitchen cupboard, find a bag of walnuts, take to the fort, share
6. Go to the kitchen cupboard, find a one pound box of raisins, take to the fort, whoops, no one here but me, heartily regret eating one pound of raisins
7. Switch to mud pies

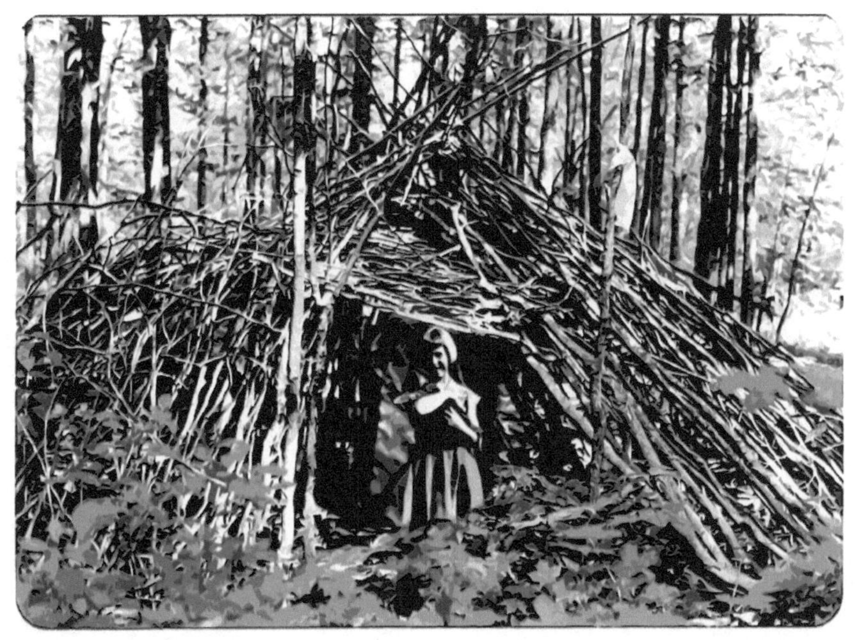

The Stick Years – rural Ontario, Canada. When my kids were little I would take them to the woods too and this is one stick fort (1980?) we built together. I had to use this representative structure because little children in the 1950s did not take cameras into the woods. That is really me during My Stick Years holding a cat and planning a kitchen raid – The Score is real history, 6 kids can never have enough snacks.

20

Brian R. Nickerson

bulk tape

a. buy 100 rolls of packing tape (clear)
b. tape all four walls, top to bottom, of apartment room

(college, (1991), Olympia, WA)

First Times

drop acid
a. - z.
eat mushrooms
z. - a.

(college, (1989 - 1990) - Austin, TX)

Suffer the Wrath...

burn the witch

a. stumble upon a gallon of gasoline
b. get your best friend
c. sneak off to side of apartment building
d. pour gasoline over each other
e. run screaming to Mommy because of the itching pain
f. get put in bath tub and doused with water
g. suffer the wrath of Mommy

pop

a. get on bus to go to kindergarten
b. have a tupperware container filled with brownies
c. pull out pencil
d. pop holes in tupperware
e. enjoy the sound
f. pop holes in bus seats
g. enjoy the sound
h. get others to do the same
i. be sent to principal/teacher
j. confess to being ringleader in bus destruction
k. suffer the wrath of Mommy

(kindergarden, (1976) - Ft. Leavenworth, KS)

teacher

a. enter first grade
b. disagree with class direction
c. place feet on top of desk
d. tell teacher that you could teach the class better than her
e. be sent to principal
f. suffer the wrath of Mommy

(1st grade, (1977) - El Paso, TX)

21

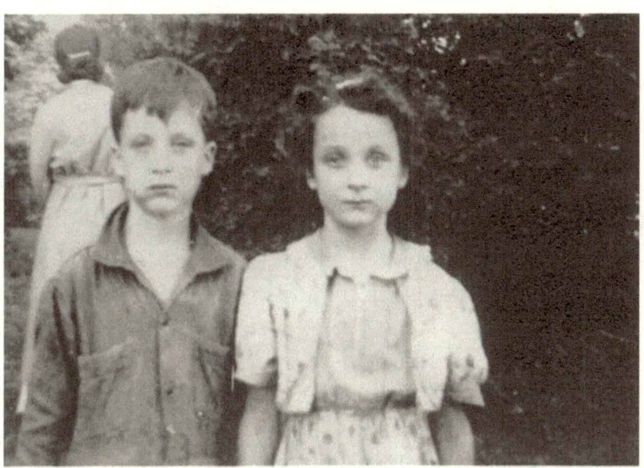

Don Boyd left and Mary – 1940 – on Beatty Farm, near Croton, Ohio. Both age six. "I call this time; 'the end of my childhood.' My Jaw looks swollen and I remember pulling my own jaw tooth with pliers from my dad's workshop about this time."

Don Boyd

At about the age of three our family was enlarged when my father remarried after my mother died in late 1935 during the 'Great Depression'. Times were hard and we lived on rented farms and grew our own produce and livestock. We combined the two families, which meant I had three older stepbrothers and a younger sister. Mary, my new younger sister, then became my constant playmate. I usually 'instigated' these activities and for the life of me, I don't know how I came up with some of them.

Ken Friendman encountered criticism for listing some of his childhood activities in his Fluxus performances. Yet, I feel that there is something to the 'nature vs. nurture' arguments. I am a professional educator and none of us claim to have all of the answers in this regard. Here then, are my early indications of unusual childhood non-conformist or 'Fluxus' activities.

Event #1

Jump on Grandpa

The idea was to run and jump on grandpa's lap as he was taking a nap on the living room sofa. Mary went first and my stepmother was alerted when I giggled at the results.

Event #2

Play in the Cow-Feed

Ground corn and oats made great fun for playing but it was easy to detect.

Event #3

Throw cornstalks down the cistern

Warning… my father was very angry at this waste of feed and contamination of our water supply. He threatened to lower me ten feet into the cistern to fish out the cornstalks. My stepmother saw him fashioning a "bosun's chair" out of his horse reins and stopped him.

Event #4

Fill the preacher's gas tank with sand.

Mary and I actually did this one Sunday afternoon while the preacher was visiting.

Event #5

Throw cornstalks at the chickens in the henhouse

We did this too, until I knocked one unconscious and quit the practice.

Event #6

Let the air out of the family automobile tires

The hissing made a great noise (or music as John Cage might have said).

Event #7

Play "King of the Mountain" on the school ash pile.

This was a favorite during first grade recess.

Event #8

Act a fool in the coatroom

I used to bang my head on the coatroom wall, and act like it was an accident to amuse the other first graders.

Event #9

Take a rag to school and tear it when the other boys bend down to play marbles.

I let them fret awhile before I told them it was a joke.

Event #10

Pretend to be drunk at the senior class hayride

I would pretend to drink hard cider then stagger alongside the wagon or fall over the fence to amuse my fellow students. (some of them insisted that I was really drunk)

22

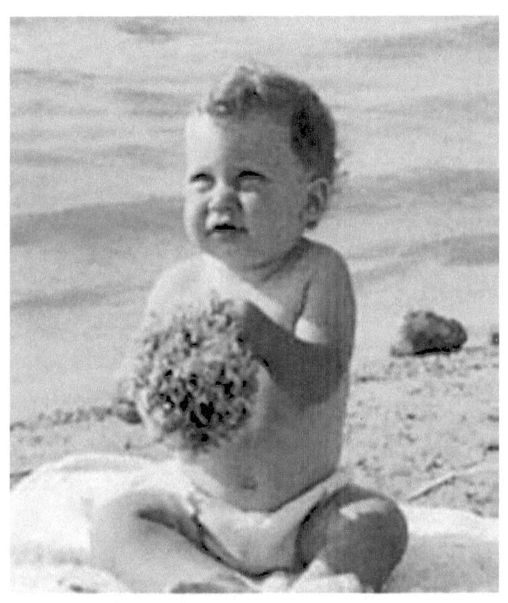

Allan Revich

Sand Event

Wear a diaper

Sit on some sand

Squeeze an old sponge

Cowboy Event

Wear a cowboy shirt

Be very handy

Laugh out loud

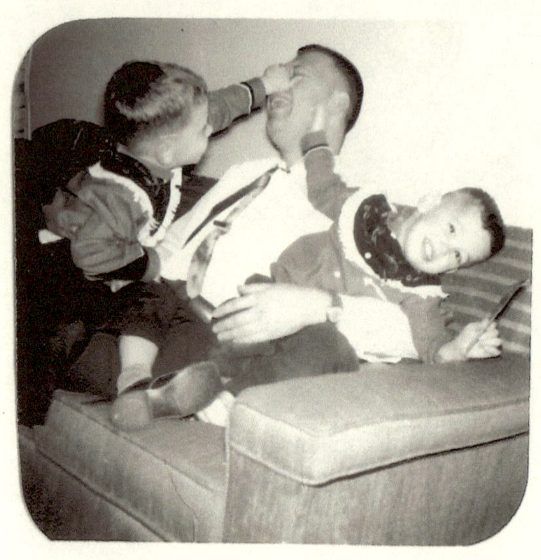

Birthday Cake Event

Place a birthday cake on a table

Sit on the same table

Act as if you did not just shit your pants

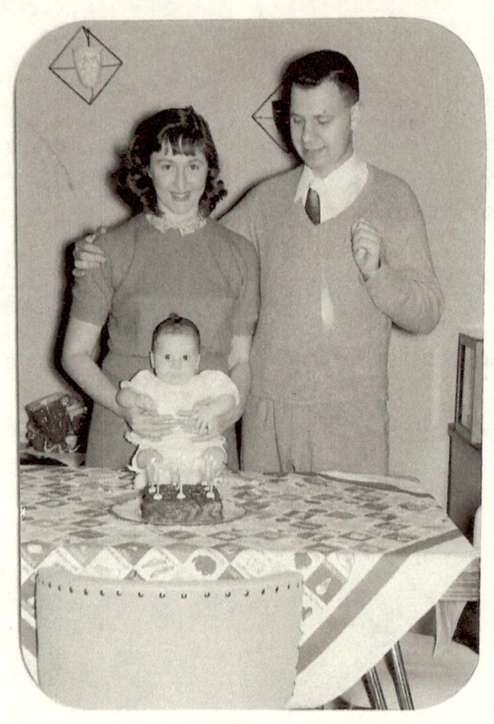

Plaid Event

Wear a plaid vest

Wear a matching bow tie

Smile at people

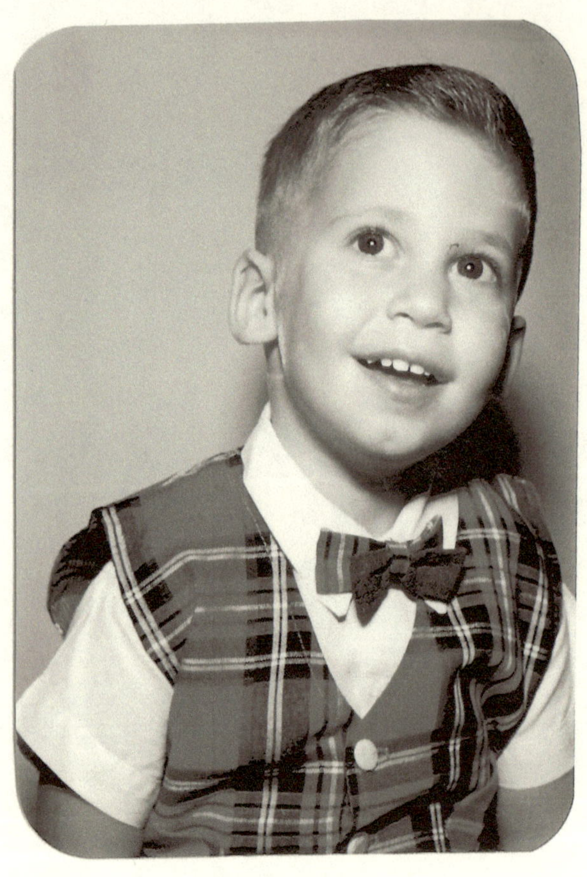

Floor Show Event

Be very small

Sit on the floor

Hold onto a test tube

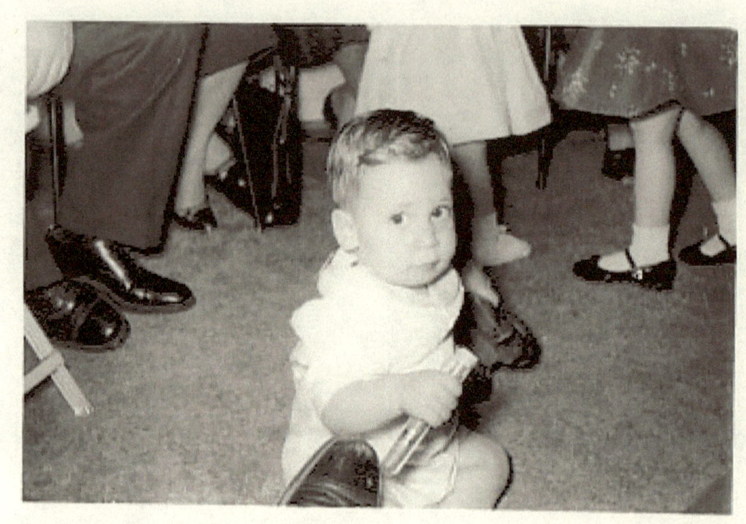

23

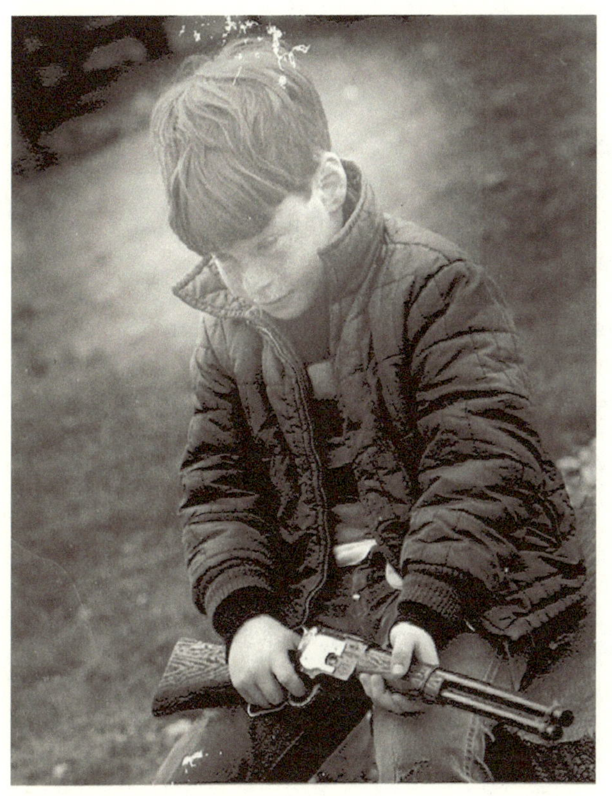

Matthew Rose

GETTING HOOKED

Eat a can of tuna fish with lemon juice
Hold your father's fish hook in your hand
Have a fight with your older brother
Accidentally put the fish hook into his thumb
Watch your father remove it
Years later reflect about fishing with Wittgenstein
Write a Fluxus score from the experience
Print it up and leave it in phone booths all over America
Be sure you remove the phone from the hook

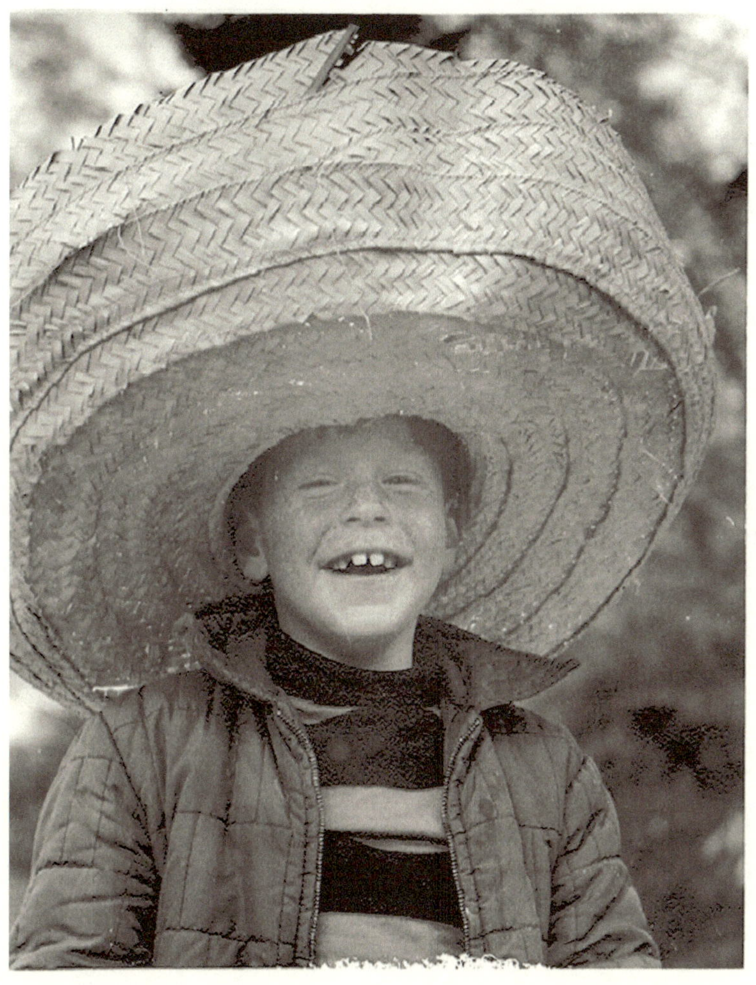

ROCK ON

Wait until you have a good cry on
Go outside and sit on a rock
Look directly at the sun
Close your eyes
With a small rock write your name into the larger rock
Open your eyes
Celebrate your birthday

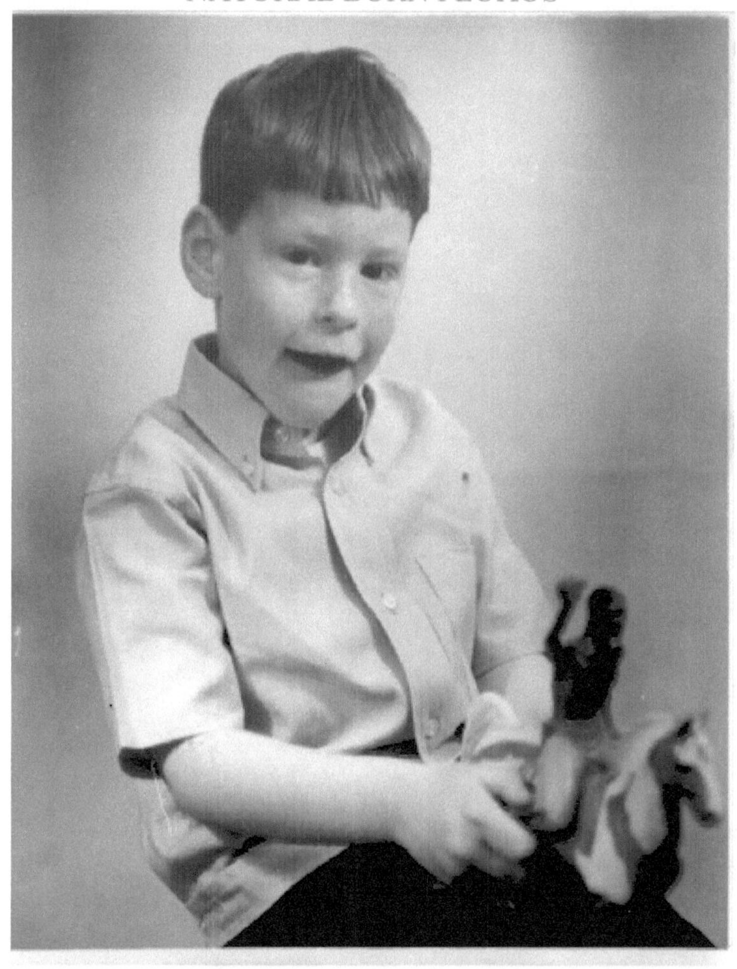

HIDE

Find a closet
Step inside
Pull the doors shut
Open your eyes
Try to see your future
Repeat once a year

OVER THE WALL

Find an umbrella
Find a high wall
Scale the wall
Stand on top of the wall
Open the umbrella
Jump into the air
Fall into the rosebushes below
Cry like there's no tomorrow

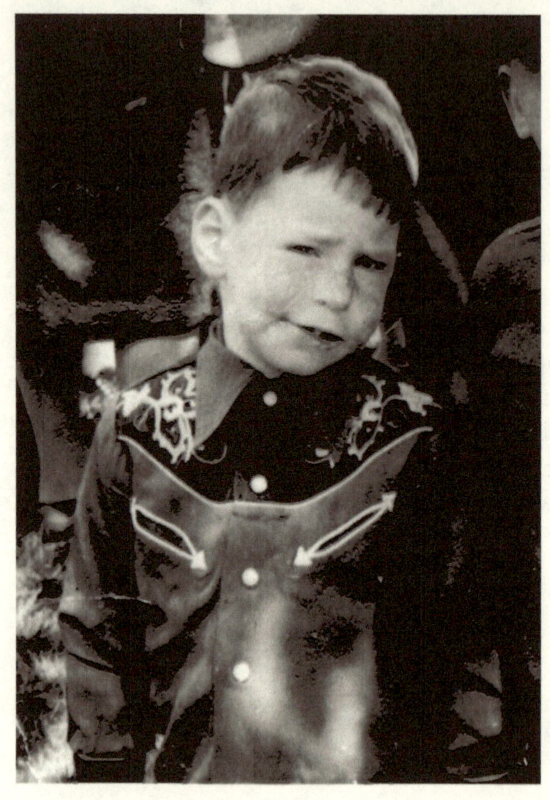

KITCHEN

Invite yourself into someone's home
Hang out, have a drink
Wait into your friends go into the bathroom
Get a big pot, fill 1/2 with water, turn on the stove
Go into the refrigerator and grab 12 edible items
Put all 12 (properly peeled or cut or opened) into the pot
Wait till your friend comes out of the bathroom
Feign ignorance, say: "What's cookin'?"

24

Peter Frank

I began writing poetry and happenings at my summer camp in the summer of 1964, at the age of 14. I was first exposed to the *Something Else Press* in the spring of 1966, shortly before turning 16. The conflation of artistic disciplines in the intermedial forms represented in and by the *Press*, reifying and expanding upon my interest in the happening, excited and challenged me.

Influenced in particular by the *Great Bear Pamphlets*, whose intimate chapbook format, low prices, and unpredictable contents charmed me, I hand-fabricated my own booklets -- a few by friends of mine, but mostly by me. The first was called *Solos For the Home*, presenting a sequence of terse performance instructions clearly modeled on the poetic diction of Fluxus scores (if somewhat more gestural in actual instruction). The second was called *Pitchy Dry*, interspersing quasi-graphic and free-word, or "language," poems (probably influenced by Jackson Mac Low and, equally, Aram Saroyan) with performance scores even more open-ended -- and poem-like -- than those in *Solos For the Home.*

I'm providing the entire contents of *Solos For the Home* and the performance-oriented works from *Pitchy Dry*. These are the earliest notations of their kind I still have in my possession.

Solos for the Home 1966

SUGGESTED AUDIENDES:
In city – Half a dozen people chosen at random off street
In suburbs – 3 little kids living on block
In small town or in country – Alone
In hotel – 1 person from room on same floor

1.

Call friend on telephone
Have friend listen to clock ticking for 20 sec.
Talk very softly in background, preferably to someone else

2.

Pad self with pillows
Take shower
Tear apart pillows
Bang on walls of shower

3.

Rummage through dresser (nervously & violently)
Stop every so often and wring hands quickly

4.

Turn on all radios, televisions and phonographs in house
Let blare for 10 min.

5.

Throw rubber bands & empty bottles out windows

6.

Scrawl epithets on walls
Occasionally shriek

7.

Read short book

8.

Lather walls of one room with shaving cream and/or whipped cream

9.

Sit silently, 5 min.

10.

Paste postage stamps to bread

11.

Pull down all window shades
Go through motions of undressing without actually removing clothing

12.

Read newspaper article out loud
Light candle

13.

Take large cardboard
Write "End"
Hold up

The following from

Pitchy Dry – poems*acts – 1966-67

INTRODUCTION

!!!!!!!!!!!!!!!!!!!!!!!!!!

!!!!!!!!!!!!!!!!!!!!!!!!!!

!!!!!!!!!!!!!!!!!!!!!!!!!!

!!!!!!!!!!!!!!!!!!!!!!!!!!

!!!!!!!!!!!!!!!!!!!!!!!!!!

!!!!!!!!!!!!!!!!!!!!!!!!!!

!!!!!!!!!!!!!!!!!!!!!!!!!!

!!!!!!!!!!!!!!!!!!!!!!!!!!

for coyote

I assumed this to be a reference to the character from the TV cartoon The Roadrunner Show - Wile E. Coyote (also known simply as "The Coyote" When I asked Peter he said:

"You mean the Warner Bros cartoon? Not deliberately, altho, along with the rest of my generation, the cartoon made a profound impression. (And I must admit to comparing Maciunas to the roadrunner and the guys -- state and Mafia -- pursuing him in the early 70s to Wile E Coyote...)"

"'by Peter Frank' by Dick Higgins" by Peter Frank
by Dick Higgins

All Higgins's Danger Musics performed simultaneously.
by Peter Frank

THANK YOU PIECE

Thank you
Thank you
Thank you
Thank you
Thank you
Thank you
Thank you
Thank you
Thank you
Thank you
Thank you
        politeness is NO crime

ASKING PIECE

Inquiry

MANIC EVENT

The other side of the moon
(Is thought about/Discussed)

ROT PIECE

Old apples

GALILEO

Thermostat in 4/4 time

DEVOTIONAL

Put part of

something

over here

Put part of

something else

over here

WEATHER MUSIC

Sounds produced in performance of Devotional

VANTAGE POINT

The Cat is No Example

HOUSE

Performance of Vantage Point with or without sneezes and audience

FESTERFISH

The New York Public Library

UNIVERSAL FISH

All libraries

LAERTES

Your back is to the door
(to be performed with back to door)

25

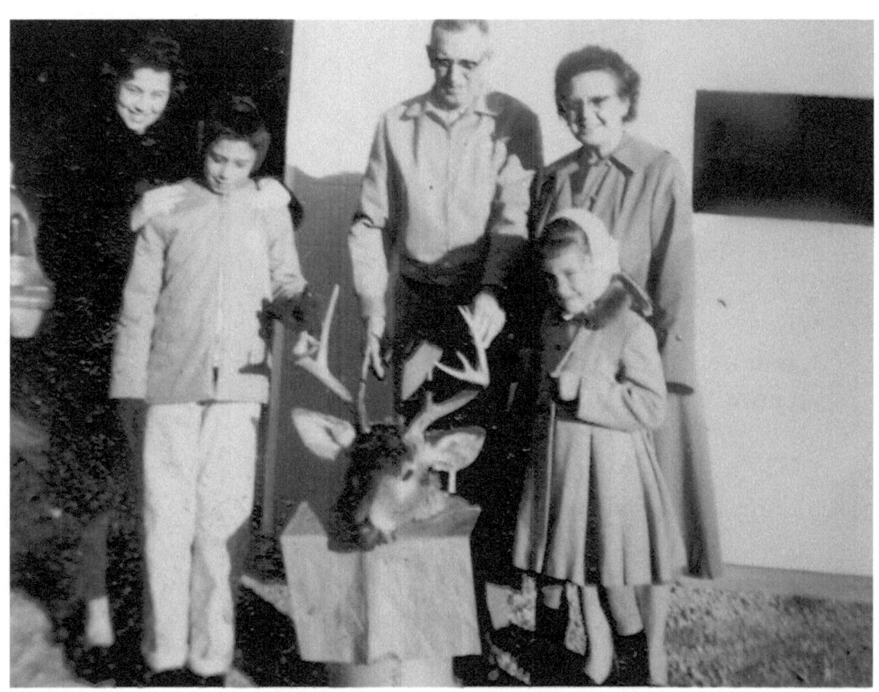

Madawg

I threw up on Santa when I was eight years old.

Throw up on Santa event

1. dress in a heavy wool coat
2.find a really long line to stand in while waiting to talk to Santa
3. make sure it is very hot in the room
4. wait until you sit on Santa's lap
5.Throw up on him after you ask for your toy

Bloomington, Indiana 1963

I was terrified Santa wouldn't come to my house because we didn't have a fire-place.

Worry about Santa

1. On Christmas Eve prepare cookies and milk for santa
2. Sit in the Livingroom waiting for Santa Claus.
3. Fret about the fact that you don't have a fire place for Santa.
4. Worry that Santa is going to skip your house
5. Hate your parents for picking the wrong house to live in.
6. Cry yourself to sleep.

Bloomington, Indiana 1963

I use to be afraid that a stinky werewolf was going to kill me in the night.

I was very jealous of my Catholic friend Chris because she got to dress up like a bride for communion. I wanted to be a bride too.

I use to love playing on the drive-in movie playground in my pajamas before it got dark

One Halloween my mom dressed me as Yogi Bear and I couldn't see out of the costume very well. Some kids and I went to a door which was answered by a werewolf. All the other kids ran away but I stayed and got candy becuase I couldn't see him.

26

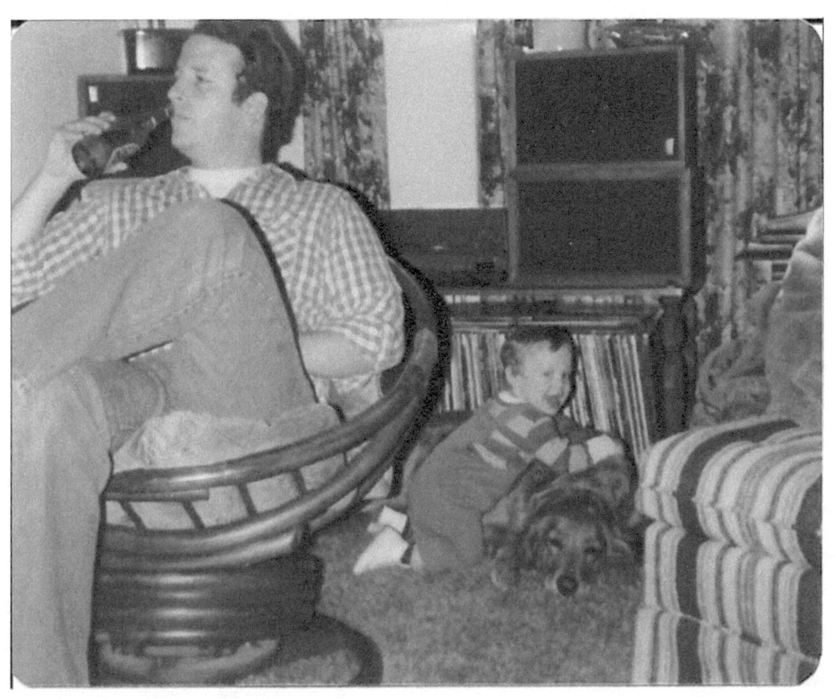

Adam Overton

DOG POOP PIECE

.

Without threatening violence,
And only through exercising your new found powers of diplomacy, salesmanship and trust,
Convince someone, preferably younger than you, and maybe even related to you, to pick up that pile of dog poop over there.
If successful, conceal your immense joy until a later age or date.

c. 1983-1984 - Norcross, Georgia

ASLEEP PIECE

.

In a non-sleeping location (i.e. the couch, floor, etc)
Fall asleep or pretend to fall asleep.

Either way, waiting for someone to pick you up - limp, with eyes closed - to place you in bed.

c. 1983-1987 - Norcross & Snellville, Georgia

DIG PIECE

.

with friends
with purpose
with shovels and/or hoes

.

Dig.

c. 1985-1988 Snellville, Georgia

ROCK PILE PREPARATION PIECE

with friends
with purpose
cussingly

.

Start a gang.

Gather and hide a decent pile of easily-hurlable rocks in an easy to access, but secret location, preferably in "the woods."
Gather and hide another pile of rocks, not too far from the first, to serve as a backup pile.
Fortify your pile-positions, perhaps with scrap metal or fallen branches that you find around the neighborhood.
Beware of older kids who might try to steal your rocks or otherwise betray you.
Rehearse a series of battle formations, as well as a series of possible endings (of both success and defeat), being careful not to hurt your own in the process.

c. 1985-1988 - Snellville, Georgia

27

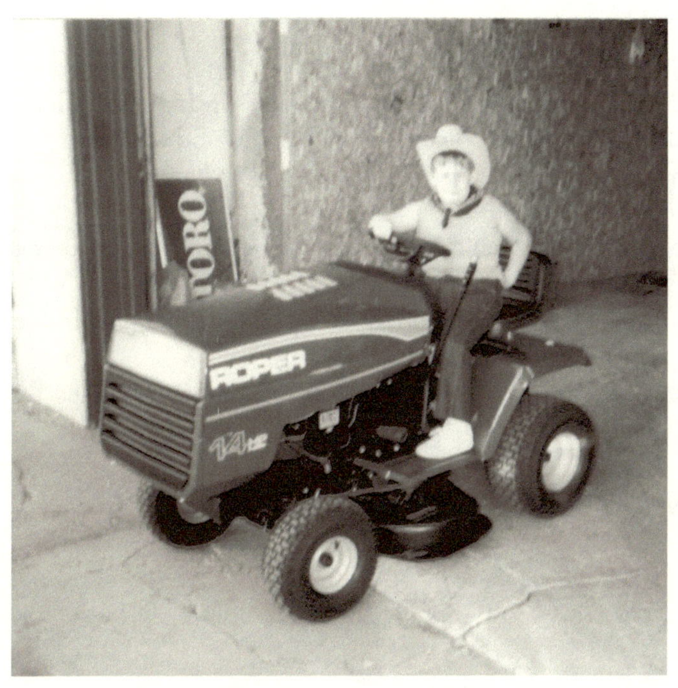

Zachary Lawrence

Sticker Event 1

1. Accumulate various stickers of cartoons, pop culture figures, etc.
2. Peel sticker; affix to piece of varnished wood furniture.
3. Repeat.

Sticker Event 2

1. Event initiates when authority figure becomes agitated at stickers on varnished wood furniture.
2. ONLY WHEN DIRECTED, use paint scraper to remove stickers.
3. Place modified varnished wood furniture in a room out of public view.

Winfield, KS – 1987

Teleport

1. Assured that no-one is watching, visualize oneself teleporting through a solid object.
2. Make noise, hand motions to signify start of teleportation.
3. Run quickly around the solid object to the other side.
4. Repeat noise, hand motions to signify successful teleportation.
5. When confronted by adult with questions, refuse to admit the truth.

Winfield, KS – 1989

Sharing

1. With no more than two others present, step inside a circle drawn on the ground.
2. Facing the onlookers, expose a par t of your body, preferably below the waist.
3. Exit the circle, trading places with a fellow participant. Repeat.
4. Giggle uncontrollably as others perform the score.

Winfield, KS - 1986

28

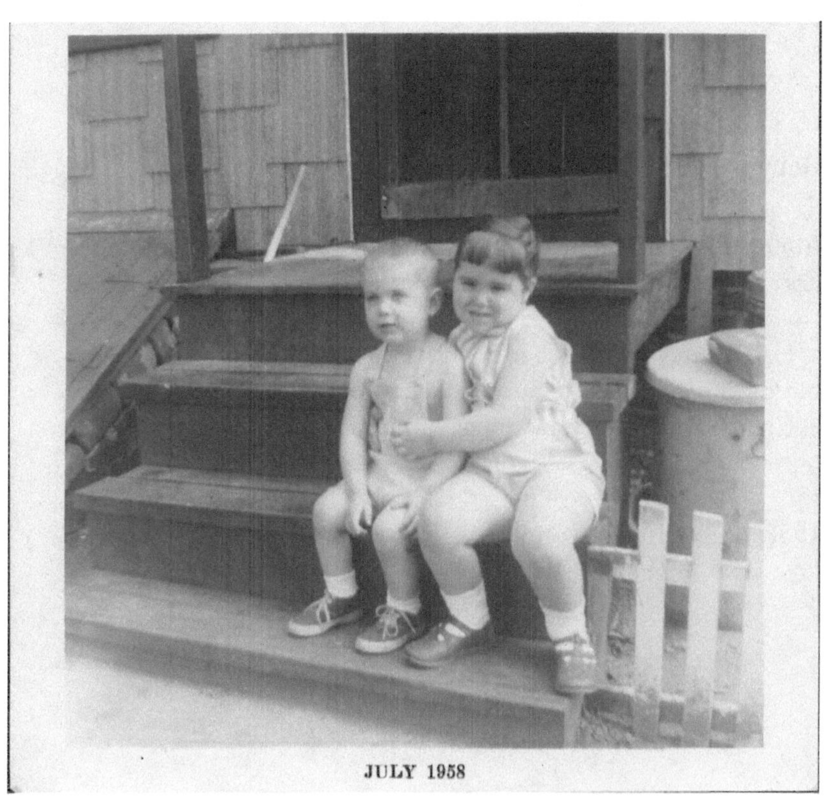
JULY 1958

Mary Campbell

Belly Rub

Interaction with audience member
Can be performed sitting or standing

a. Use whatever word is in your head
b. Put one arm around audience member
c. Chant word and rub audience members belly

1958, New Britain, Conn. U.S.

29

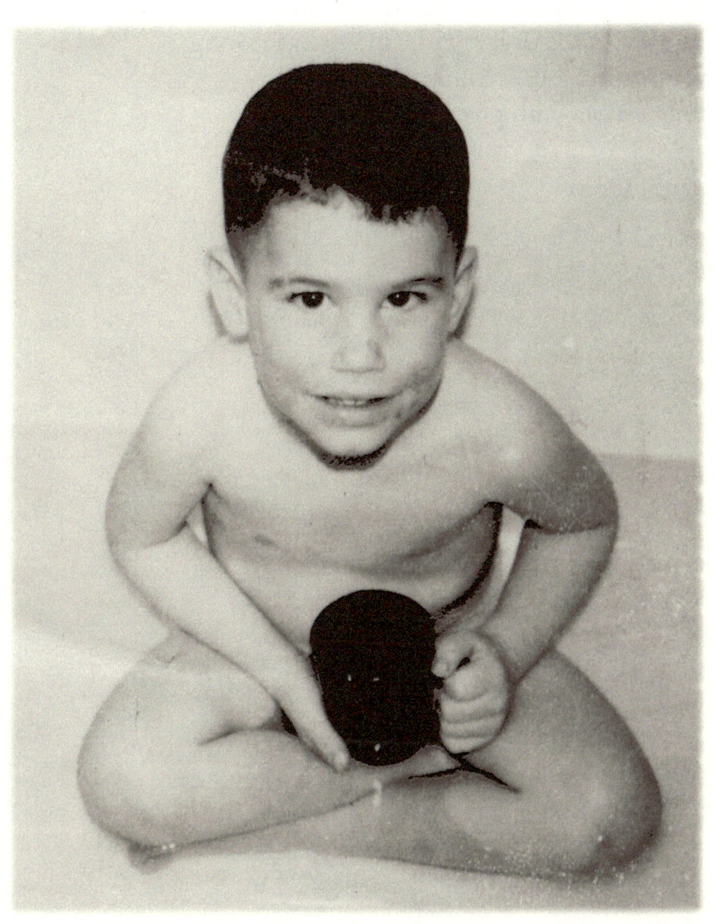

Mark Bloch

Value Added Gift Event (1960)

1. Grandmother presents one dollar bill to grandson.
2. Grandson takes dollar and runs to bathroom.
3. Grandson flushes bill down the toilet.
4. Family erupts with glee.

Cleveland, Ohio

Mysterious Erotic Event (1962)

1. Apply glue, paste or other adhesive to thumb and first finger.
2. Press thumb and finger together, allow partial drying.
3. Slowly pull thumb and finger apart, showing colleague in profile.
4. Smile mysteriously.

Cleveland, Ohio

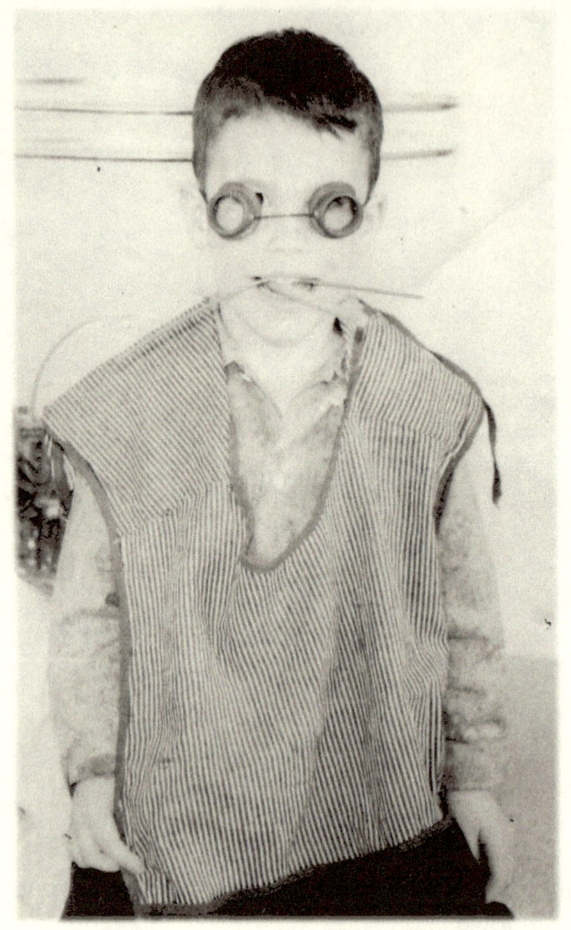

Mark Bloch

Danger Music Bus Event for Larry B. (1967)

1. Enter bus.
2. Scream.

Cleveland, Ohio

Danger Music Bus Event for Denise C. (1963)

1. Enter bus.
2. Cry.

Cleveland, Ohio

Mysterious Erotic Event for Richard Bloch (1961)

1. Open any found Playboy Magazine to centerfold on flat surface.
2. Fully open centerfold.
3. Leave.

Cleveland, Ohio

Off Color Event for Art Teacher for Doris Gruber (1966)

1. Fuck the music teacher.

Cruelty Event for Doris Gruber (1965)

During exciting art making event, make someone else stand in hall.

Cleveland, Ohio

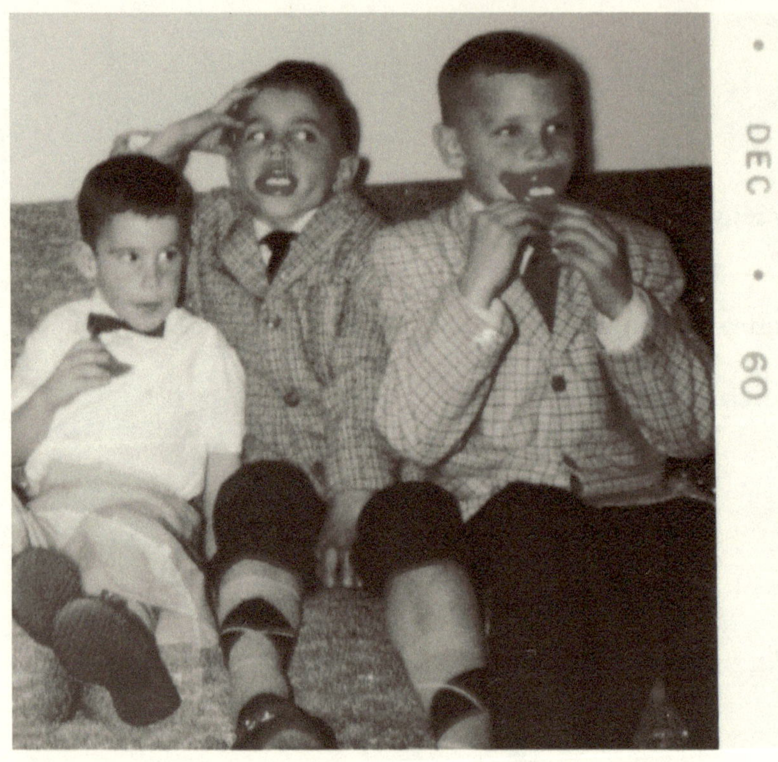

Mark Bloch

Art Making Nothing for Ray Johnson (1965)

During exciting art making event, stand in hall.

Cleveland, Ohio

Buddy Event (1961-74)

1. Close door to bedroom.
2. Lie on bed or floor.
3. Holding object above head, create fantasy in mind, manipulate object rapidly.
4. Provide sound effects with mouth as needed.

Cleveland, Ohio

Sleep More Event (1969)

1. Wake up.
2. Enter bathroom, lock door.
3. Lie on floor.
4. Sleep more.

Cleveland, Ohio

Perfect Circle Event (1963)

(each step should be said aloud as it is being done)

1. Take a piece of bread.
2. Fold it.
3. Bite it.
4. Open it.
5. You have a hole.

Cleveland, Ohio

30

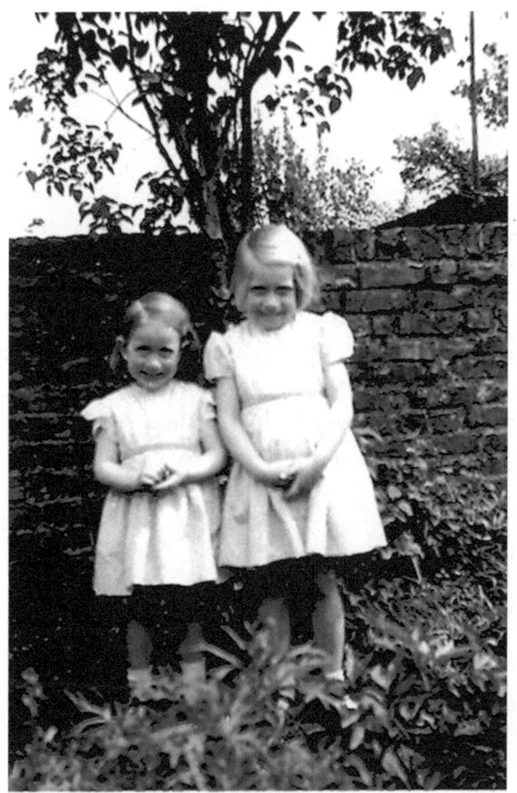

Roger and his sisters, Sally and Karen. Unfortunately Roger was daydreaming and arrived just too late to be in the picture.

Roger Stevens

DOCUMENTATION

You might wish to document the following pieces or you might not. It's enough to have performed them. You might like to dream up your own method of documentation. This could include taking photos, having a friend or accomplice film you or writing an email to those involved the following day.

Daydreaming

When I was about nine I set off for a music lesson and arrived fifteen minutes late. The house was only a five minute walk away. Daydreaming, I guess. Another time around the same age I came home from school during the morning break, thinking it was dinner time. I spent a lot of time as a child in that daydreaming otherworldly place.

Arriving Late

Arrange with a friend or colleague to meet them at a certain time and place. The place should be between a five and fifteen minute walk away.
Sort out when you need to leave to arrive with time to spare.
Leave for your appointment but spend the time thinking about anything other than the journey you are on. Walk slowly. Take in the sights. Stop for a chat. Arrive about fifteen minutes late.

Unexpected Break

This needs to be performed at a place of work. If you have no job or work for yourself you will need to precede this piece with Un-expected Break (Pre-Performance Piece)

At work. When you have your normal mid-morning break instead of visiting the water cooler, coffee bar, canteen or smoking corner – go home. At home have a cup of coffee and then return to work. If anyone asks where you were – explain that you got the time wrong.

Unexpected Break (Pre-Performance Piece)

Get a job.

31

Matthew Taggart

In looking back at my creative progression I've realised that I've haven't veered to far off of the path I've consciencely taken years ago. actually its been there since the beginning. from the time I was performed devo as a three year old with a record player to the noise experiments I did before I was aware of the noise scene. The surrealist poems of my teens and so forth. Its been there. For me, creativity has been about change and progress. I was never interested in a certain genre or approach. They all have benefits. I always enjoyed a good joke at the expense of art and music. I saw it all useful and useless at the same time. That's what made it fun for me the flexibility that was there but no one would admit to. The seriousness of it all turned me off. I take my creative process very serious as we all should but the importance is what you don't take serious. It can all come crashing in on you if you put too much emphasis on it. You can't take it with you when you die. I think it was more pure as a child for me cause I wasn't aware of the process like I am now. If fluxus is about harnessing the unconscience then fluxus only exsisted when I was between the ages of three to six years old. After that it became a chase for that experience.

Bird Song

whistle along with the birds in your neighborhood.

try and mimic their song with the intention of communicating with them.

if more than one bird is singing make up your own part to harmonize with them

Record Party

aquire a copy of Devo's Freedom of Choice lp.
dress up in toddler's clothes
play the record and sing along with Whip It

*perform this in front of your immediate family

event was realized around 1980-1981 in Cody Wyoming

Notes on Contributors

Several of the contributors to this work were selected to publish an essay as one of eleven contemporary "New Fluxus" artists who are seen to *'inhabit the site of Fluxus, developing and interpreting the Fluxus tradition in a new way.'* in a special double issue of the journal *Visible Language* on Fluxus. The double issue was developed by Owen Smith and Ken Friedman and published through the Rhode Island School of Design. The artists included as representing New Fluxus artists: Alan Bowman, **Bibiana Padilla Maltos**, David-Baptiste Chirot, David Cologiovani, Eryk Salvaggio, **Cecil Touchon**, mIEKAL aND, MTAA, **Litsa Spathi**, Sol Nte, and **Walter Cianciusi**.

Peter Frank

PETER FRANK is Senior Curator at the Riverside Art Museum, Associate Editor for THEmagazineLA, and, until recently, critic for Angeleno magazine and the
L. A. Weekly. He was born in 1950 in New York, where he served as art critic for The Village Voice and The SoHo Weekly News, and moved to Los Angeles in 1988, where he edited VISIONS art quarterly in the early 1990s. Frank contributes articles to numerous publications and has written many monographs and catalogues to one-person and group exhibitions. Frank has also organized numerous theme and survey shows, most notably "19 Artists – Emergent Americans," the 1981 Exxon National Exhibition mounted at the Guggenheim Museum. McPherson & Co.-Documentext published his Something Else Press: An Annotated Bibliography in 1983. A cycle of poems, The Travelogues, was issued by Sun & Moon Press in 1982. Abbeville Press released New, Used & Improved, an overview of the New York art scene co-written with Michael McKenzie, in 1987. Frank has also published many catalogues and artists' monographs, including Roller: The Paintings of Donald Roller Wilson, for Chronicle Books in 1988 and Robert De Niro, Sr., for Salander-O'Reilly in 2004.

John M. Bennett

As well as steadily producing and distributing his own work, Bennett, through "Luna Bisonte Prods", a small press founded in 1974, has published thousands of limited edition items by writers who compose visual poetry, word art, and other experimental fiction/art/poetry. Bennett's papers, and published works, as well as the results of his own publishing activities (including 30 years of "Lost & Found Times" magazine), are collected in several major institutions, including Washington University (St. Louis), SUNY Buffalo, The Ohio State University and The Museum of Modern Art.

Bennett has won the attention of critic Richard Kostelanetz and other commentators on the avant-garde.

Bennett himself is the curator of the "Avant Writing Collection", "The William Burroughs Collection", and "The Cervantes Collection" at the Ohio State University Libraries. More information about Bennett's career, publishing activities and artistic endeavors can be found at his website.

Bennett has performed solo and with numerous musicians and other poets, often with the collaborative sound poetry group *THE BE BLANK CONSORT*, which has released a recording titled *SOUND MESS*. This group was founded as a result of a symposium organized by Richard Kostelanetz at the Atlantic Center for the Arts in 1999. The members of *THE BE BLANK CONSORT* include Scott Helms, Carlos Luis, and Kathy Ernst, among others.
Web: www.johnmbennett.net/

Don Boyd

My short bio is that I now teach design, sculpture and advanced photography at Mt. Vernon, Ohio, University. I met Ken Friedman while teaching at South Dakota University in April, 1975. We have been friends and correspondents since. I met Dick Higgins, Allison Knowles, and George Maciunas in 1976 when I spent the summer on the Higgins farm near Barton, Vermont. I catalogued Dick's performances upt to that time. I also wrote 50 CHARACTERISTICS OF FLUXUS from that experience. In 1978 Ken named me Director of Fluxus West.
Web: http://donaldboyd.blogspot.com/

Adam Overton

Adam Overton (b. 1979) is a composer, performer, teacher and massage therapist living in Los Angeles.
Web: plus1plus1plus.org/

Madawg

my bio:

I knew I didn't believe in God when in the 4th grade I saw a picture of God towering over some skyscraper in the hallway of my church.

I have since lived by the seat of my pants and still have survived.

I was on Oprah.

I called myself the "world's most famous unknown artist" until I found out Ray Johnson and Yoko Ono did the same.

I am John Held Jr's stalker.

He likes the attention.

My most recent fluxus event: I bought a 60's Fluxus poster from John Held Jr. for $250.00--it is worth thousands--he has no idea.

Ruud Janssen

A Dutch Fluxus and mail artist currently living in Breda in the Netherlands.

Ruud Janssen studied Physics and Mathematics. He became active with mail art in 1980 and did several international mail art projects. From 1994 till 2001 he has conducted interviews with Fluxus and mail artists in different communication forms; the results have been published in booklets and on the internet since 1996. In later years he focused more on acrylic painting and individual correspondences. He always maintains his site with the latest details of his work.

Janssen publishes articles, magazines and booklets with his TAM-Publications and participates in international mail art projects, collaborations and exhibitions. He founded IUOMA (International Union of Mail-Artists) in 1988 and is also the curator of the *TAM-Rubberstamp Archive*, the result of a Mail Art collection that has been accumulated by him from 1983 till now. The archive contains prints, original rubberstamps, magazines and literature. It is the longest time a mail art project has run ever (details see link to latest online catalogue). In 1994 he started with his Mail-interviews which have been published as booklets and online. The interviews have a new concept where the question is sent in a specific communicationform and the interviewed person chooses his own way to get the answer back. This way the factor time is involved in each specific interview. Samples of interviewed persons are: Ray Johnson, Dick Higgins, Ken Friedman, Anna Banana, Mark Bloch, Patricia Tavenner, Michael Leigh, Alison Knowles and Guy Bleus.
http://www.iuoma.org/index.html

In 2003 Litsa Spathi founded together with Ruud Janssen the Fluxus Heidelberg Center for which they are building up a collection of Fluxus material and where they also publish their own works.

Sheila E. Murphy

Sheila E. Murphy was born in Mishawaka, Indiana, and has lived most of her adult life in Phoenix, Arizona, where she is a poet and visual poet. She regularly performs her work and is an active collaborator. Murphy has straddled the worlds of art and business all her life, and leads a successful consulting firm devoted to Executive Development.

Published Works to Date

- *Collected Chapbooks*. Blue Lion Books. 2008.
- *Parsings*. Arrum Press (Finland). 2008.
- *The Case of the Lost Objective Case*. Otoliths Press. 2007.
- *Continuations* (with Douglas Barbour). The University of Alberta Press, 2006.
- *Incessant Seeds*. Pavement Saw Press, 2005.
- *Proof of Silhouettes*. Stride Press (UK), 2004.
- *Concentricity*. Pleasure Boat Studio: A Literary Press, 2004.
- *Green Tea with Ginger*. Potes & Poets Press, 2003.
- *Letters to Unfinished J*. Green Integer Press, 2003.
- *The Stuttering of Wings*. Stride Press (UK), 2002.
- *The Indelible Occasion*. Potes & Poets Press, 2000.
- *Falling in Love Falling in Love With You Syntax: Selected and New Poems*. Potes & Poets Press, 1997.
- *A Clove of Gender*. Stride Press (UK), 1995.
- *Pure Mental Breath*. Gesture Press (Toronto), 1994.
- *Tommy and Nell*. Sun/Gemini Press (Tucson, Arizona), 1993.
- *Teth*. Chax Press, 1991.
- *Sad Isn't the Color of the Dream*. Stride Press (UK), 1991.
- *With House Silence*. Stride Press (UK), 1987.

Litsa Spathi

(born 1958) is a Greek artist, performer and Fluxus inspired artist, currently living in Heidelberg, Germany and Breda, Netherlands. She makes collages, object books, Fluxus poetry and large acrylic paintings.

Litsa Spathi has been a revolutionary artist working for at least three decades in the art genre referred to as fantastic realism. She is the co-founder of the history making Fluxus Heidelberg Center with collaborator Ruud Janssen in 2003. She is a painter and performance artist, mail artist and writer of Fluxus poetry, a style of poetry which goes beyond words and becomes Visual Poetry. In this art form the writer/artist uses letters and words to make visual images, some call it collages of texts, to make a message clear for the viewer. The roots of Visual Poetry lies in the art-forms DaDa and Bauhaus technique. Litsa Spathi has been a contributor to art magazines internationally as well as to several group exhibitions and solo-exhibitions. Her work is found at Kunstförderung in Baden-Württemberg. She travels extensively to various European countries for her art and also teaches for the Fluxus Heidelberg Center fluxusheidelberg.org. Her works are found in several national and international archives, museums and private collections. The archives at the Fluxus Heidelberg Center are extensive with the intent to document, celebrate and keep the Fluxus spirit and movement alive. The performances which are too vast to mention here can be found on the website and include luminaries such as Yoko Ono, Ken Friedman, BuBu, Ben Vautier, Geoffrey Hendricks, Alison Knowles, Nam June Paik, Larry Miller, John M. Bennett, to mention a few. The Fluxus art movement was first started by such artists as George Maciunas, John Cage, Dick Higgins, George Brecht and Allan Kaprow. Please see the site for the Fluxus Heidelberg Center's latest events and merchandise/artwork such as the 'Standards and warrantees' themed stickers, and Fluxus Poetry Cards and Fluxus bucks and limited edition ATC, calendar of events, various chapbooks and essays. They have an extensive library of Fluxus poetry available for viewing. Litsa Spathi is not only cataloging, collecting and archiving Fluxus history but is creating the history in this art as well.

In 2007 Spathi founded Fluxlist Europe as a performance. This is a digital platform for Fluxus artists and visual poets to publish their work and to discuss the new and old Fluxus.

Web: www.openfluxus.com/ & fluxlisteurope.blogspot.com/

Gregory Steel

Gregory Steel was born in Detroit Michigan and raised by his maternal grandparents in the richly diverse ethnic neighborhoods of the Motor City's East Side. From an early age, Steel was encouraged by his creative grandmother to explore his artistic abilities. During his childhood he was inspired by his grandmother's innovative use of ordinary materials in constructing unique objects and arrangements. Her novel approaches to environmental resources combined with her support were a positive influence in Steel's artistic development. As a self-taught artist, Steel held jobs in various disciplines in order to support his work, but after many years of making art on his own he realized he needed a serious arts education.

Attending school part-time and working full-time, Steel received a BFA from The College for Creative Studies in Detroit Michigan, and an MFA in art from the University of Michigan. After his studies were completed he took a position at The College for Creative Studies teaching sculpture and experimental media. Steel is currently an assistant professor at Indiana University where his courses are concentrated in sculpture and new media.

The art of ideas is fundamental to Steel's working process and is at the heart of his work to date. For Steel, art and life are not separate spheres. Instead, his art is only an extension of who he is, and thus is fully integrated into his life. Navigating academic discourse and the Modernist dilemma, Steel soon came to depend on his instinct that art is an internal process. His influences include Marcel Duchamp, Joseph Beuys, Lawrence Weiner and Allan Kaprow. Experience, rather than individual created objects, is foremost in Steel's work. To this end, Steel employs a variety of materials and techniques in his art, including video, object making, digital imaging, book publishing, installation, performance and new technology. As an idea artist, he views the various materials he uses as simply a way to fulfill the function of the art. Through this diversity, he resists easy categorization. Steel's work cannot be pigeon-holed because it is integrated with his life, and as such, it is a richly layered and evolving experience.

In 1994, a brush with cancer gave him a greater appreciation of life and has affected his work in ways that give him a greater focus and sense of urgency to complete his life's work. His concerns about issues of the human condition and social change, and his hope for humankind, are evident regardless of his final product. Whether Steel is collaborating in a ground-breaking physiological monitoring system with Cybernet Systems of Ann Arbor, or creating intimate and humorous tableaus replete with miniature figures in outlandish settings, his art emerges as thoughtful and timely. Steel's work has been exhibited across the United States and Europe, most recently in China, Russia, London, and in Barcelona, Spain.

Christine Tarantino

Wendell, Massachusetts USA
Born 1948, 3 December, New York City

Tarantino is an Italian-American Fluxus artist creating works of visio-textual art in the style of Arte Povera, and now publishing her eleventh artist book collection of international mail artists' works. Her visio-textual art includes: concrete/visual poetry; collage, using organic/found materials; mail art, a global artist network of collaborations and correspondence in which art moves through mail as its medium; and artist books, unique and small editions of original writings/images in artistic book-related structures.

Tarantino creates mixed-media works with the energy, ideas, and materials she has at THE MOMENT; innovation and experimentation with primary interest in the forces of nature. She regularly exhibits in mail art shows throughout the world. She joined Dodo/Dada ARTE POSTALE, and enjoys to comunicando in italiano. Recently she joined OPEN FLUXUS and continues to meet artists who are also pushing the boundaries. Visit Words of Light MAIL ART at www.ChristineTarantino.blogspot.com...to Fluxus/Mail Art; one beautiful family of artists cooperating, communicating, corresponding...

Lorraine Kwan

I was born at the end of WW11 to an English war bride and a Canadian pilot. We set up house in Ottawa where my short-lived stint as princess came to a quick end as I soon became the eldest of 6. We led a grand life in the country raiding my mother's pantry and running like a pack of wild dogs. Toys hold no interest when you can make whatever you want out of scraps, sticks and string.

Allan Revich

Born 1956 in Toronto, Canada

Studied art at the University of Toronto, the Ontario College of Art, and the Jerusalem Printmaking Workshop.

Graduated from the University of Toronto with a Bachelor of Arts degree and a Master of Education degree from the Ontario Institute for Studies in Education.

My work has been exhibited in group shows in Toronto, the United States, and Israel, and is currently on exhibit in several online galleries. Examples of my work are in several private and public collections worldwide. My Poetry has appeared in several small press publications. Two volumes of conceptual Haiku, a book of visual poetry have also been published.

Artist's Statement:

I am interested in the conceptual basis for art. What is art? Does art have to be beautiful? Does it have to be meaningful, and if so to whom? In my artwork I explore these and other issues around semiotics, poetics and visual representation. My work draws on many influences, ranging from the concept drawings of Leonardo da Vinci to the visual explorations of artists like Marcel Duchamp, Claude Monet, John Cage, Andy Warhol, Ray Johnson, George Maciunas, and Jenny Holzer. My work is also influenced by social, political, and postmodern theoretical discourse. For the last several years I have aligned myself closely with Fluxus and Intermedia. I contribute frequently to the Fluxlist and the Fluxlist Blog.

Matthew Rose

Matthew Rose (1959 -) is an artist and writer based in Paris. His most recent exhibitions were called *THE END OF THE WORLD, A KICK IN THE KUNST, SPELLING WITH SCISSORS, THE WHOLE TRUTH and PLANTING CUTING FLOWERS*. He has written for THE NEW YORK TIMES, ART & ANTIQUES, entrée, ART REVIEW and many other magazines on art and culture.

He's an artist, he says, "Because I like the hours."

Favorite quotes: "My karma ran over my dogma."

His web site: http://homepage.mac.com/mistahcoughdrop/

Cecil Touchon

Born in 1956 in Austin, Texas, Touchon grew up from kindergarden through community college in the suburbs of Saint Louis, Missouri. In 1977 at the age of twenty-one he moved to Fort Worth, Texas where he had spent many of his childhood summer vacations staying with his grandparents.
Between the years 1977 and 1989 Touchon married, had two children while working as a housepainter and developing his artistic career. In 1987 Touchon co-founded the International Post-Dogmatist Group. From 1990 – 2005 Touch remarried, had his third child and lived in Pagosa Springs, Colorado, then seven years in Cuernavaca, Mexico, In 2005 Touchon relocated to Fort Worth, Texas once again where he currently lives and works.

In 1996 Touchon founded the The Ontological Museum and soon after the International Museum of Collage, Assemblage and Construction.

Touchon, aside from the Natural Born Fluxus scores found in this book, has been working parallel to Fluxus since 1975. He became involved with the Fluxus community in 1999 via the Fluxlist email community.

Reid Wood

(Gordon) Reid Wood (AKA State of Being, b.1948) is an American artist who works in a variety of media including collage, digital imaging, artist books and artistamps. He has been a participant in the Mail-Art network since 1981, and his works are in numerous Mail-Art archives around the world. He is currently Associate Professor of Art at Lorain County Community College in Elryia, Ohio.

Publications:

Robert Rauschenberg: lithographs and other related works, 1962-1970. [Oberlin, O., 1972]
Unusual people unusual places / Reid Wood. [Oberlin, Ohio] : R. Wood, [19]87. – Artist Book
Passport : state of being / Gordon Reid Wood, Jr. [1988] – Artist Book
The sacred & the profane. [1989?] – Artist Book
Codex ontologicus. Oberlin : State of Being Digital Press, 2003
Ray Johnson in Norway: State of Being Digital Press, 2003
E-flux poem : an ongoing epic : composed of subject lines from SPAM (unsolicited e-mail). Oberlin, OH : State of Being Digital Press, 2004

Luc Fierens

Luc Fierens (born 1961) lives (with his wife Annina Van Sebroeck) in Weerde (a small village between Antwerp & Brussels) near Mechelen, where they lived for 8 years .
He lives in Flandres, Belgium but he calls himself a Belgian artist to overcome the problems between the Flemish & Wallon community .
During his artistic career he has published several visual poetrybooks. He edited a poetry magazine Parallel (1982 - 1988) & started the Postflux-postbooklets in 1987.

"Luc Fierens is an active mail-artist since 1984, when he began delivering his distinctive flavor of
poesia-visiva-inspired visual poetry to individuals, exhibitions, and archives around the planet. His method of production is collage, a particular brand of verbo-visual collage that makes it points by abrupt collocations of disparate fragments of image and word. " (Geof Huth 2007)

End of 2006 he published his book "visual writing re-connected" which provides a solid overview of his work .see review of g.huth : dbqp.blogspot.com/2007/01/panem-et-circenses.html

Luc Fierens website: www.vansebroeck.

Brad Brace

The paradigmatic-shift of the so-called, Second Renaissance, is sentient. The era of the orthodox career-artist is quickly drawing to a close, as closeted, behemoth cultural institutions appear increasingly implausible and incestuous. For many creative people, the art-object has become an ingredient or inceptive aspect of a larger, open, often mediated, concern. No longer the exclusive privileged domain of the traditional alliance of dealer-academic-museum (the curatorial class), art now regularly escapes these constraints. The archaic practice of art-object-making serves personal philosophical and nascent purposes; for myself, it`s an intriguing balance of obsession, critical reflection, precision and impulsiveness. The physicality of some of my art is a gratifying counterpoint to my media-oriented and technological projects -- stirring of electrons. Predictably, the critical, avant-garde dialogue that informed my early creative work has become fractured and depreciated. Insightful intelligence is now less likely to be dependent on hierarchical scholasticism. This dethronement of learning can be understood as the most exciting intellectual frontier we are now crossing. The relevant artist today is multi-dimensional-- an intradisciplinary generalist, with an expansive set of skills.

http://bbrace.net/bbrace2.html

Mary Campbell

A visual artist for over 20 years, Mary Campbell began the performance "Sitting and Knitting" in 2001 at the request to make a piece for the first "Day de Dada" Performance Art Event.

"Sitting and Knitting" is an ongoing creation in public and private of a continual piece of knitting. It is presently 9 1/2" wide and over 90 feet long. Began as a comment on competition in society, the performance evolved to a contemplation of the passage of time and diligence of life as viewers questions of the piece were about time factors- how long has it taken to knit so far, how long will it continue?

Most of her visual artwork originates from a combination of life events and an interest in how our society shapes ideas.

Active in the East Village Art scene of the 80's she was included in many gallery shows and did several window installations. Sharing studio space in the 2B Gas Station (Second Street and Avenue B, NYC), she curated several shows there and created a 6 foot wooden human heart sculpture on the studio grounds.

Born in New Britain, Ct in 1955, she received a BFA from Pratt Institute in Brooklyn, NY. and remained in NYC, moving to Staten Island in the late 80's. She is presently a Snug Harbor Cultural Center Studio Artist, and an organizing member of "Day de Dada" a fluxus based, dada inspired Performance Art Collective.
Myspace page- www.myspace.com/knittermary

Bibiana Padilla Maltos

Poet and conceptual artist closely tie to the Fluxus movement. Co-founder of projects A.V. TEXT-FEST and A.V. TEST-PRESS. Padilla-Maltos has realised exhibitions, performances, residences and interventions in Mexicali, Tijuana, City of Mexico, Havana, San Diego, Los Angeles, San Francisco, Paris, Rome, Madrid; and the Universities of UABC, Georgia, Berkeley, San Diego, National University and La Habana. Padilla-Maltos has curated exhibitions and collaborated with Allan McCollum, David Matlin, Luke Chue and Roberto Quaglia to mention a few. Her work is quite ample, and goes from collage and the revindication of classic performances and metadramas of the Fluxus movement, to the exploration of parallel visual narratives to literary and political texts, as well as the investigation on the sense of the body in the contemporary societies.

Zachary Scott Lawrence

Zachary Scott Lawrence is a teacher and writer from Wichita, KS. He grew up in the nearby rural community of Winfield, and attended college at Kansas State University, studying literature and education. Previous works include poetry readings in the Kansas area and publications in volume 2, no. 2 & 3 of *Apocryphal Text* and in the anthology *Keepers of the Pen.*

Brian R. Nickerson

born March 31, 1971 (El Paso, TX), to Robert and Beverly Nickerson. (Army brat)

from El Paso, Texas to Omaha, Nebraska, to Columbus, Ohio, to Leavenworth, Kansas, back to El Paso, Texas.

1st to 6th grade: El Paso, Texas
7th to 9th grade: Naples, Italy
10th to 12th grade: El Paso, Texas

University of Texas at Austin
Evergreen State College
University of Texas at El Paso

No degree.

Nickerson spent some time living in a park, in Austin, until his parents rescued him and then back to El Paso. Nickerson was diagnosed, February 11, 1997: Paranoid Schizophrenic. With help, Nickerson obtained an apartment and fell into the internet and environs, hard.
Nickerson has been involved in different projects, begun and ended, paused and aborted, restarted again.

Eric KM Clark

Victoria, BC native Eric KM Clark is a Los Angeles-based composer and performer of extremely broad reach. Compositionally, his work ranges from writing for hearing and sight-deprived performers (through which he explores the indeterminate fluctuation of individual tempo and sensation vs. a mass of individuals, and the resultant harmonies and timbres) to improvisational works for his bands in North America and Europe. In downtown Los Angeles, Mr. Clark recently co-founded and co-directs a space for experimental arts, along with fellow composer Michael Winter, called *'the wulf.'*. There, they strive to provide a location for their fellow artists, as well as themselves, to present any work of experimental creative pursuit. *www.thewulf.org*

As a performer, Mr. Clark has attained wide acclaim performing works for violin composed by his contemporaries (such as his *Simplified Violin* project for which he commissioned 8 US composers to write pieces involving a violin strung with all four strings of the same gauge). He has performed in projects with a wide array of composers, including Jennifer Walshe, Travis Just, eldritch Priest, Christian Kesten, Harris Wulfson, James Orsher, Michael Pisaro, Tristan Perich, Adam Overton, and the aforementioned Mr. Winter, among many others. Mr. Clark is currently violinist for *The California E.A.R. Unit*, and a regular contributor to the *neithernor* and *Object Collection* ensembles. *www.erickmclark.com*

Walter Cianciusi

born in Tagliacozzo (AQ), Italy in 1978. In 2004 he graduated in guitar from the Conservatory "A.Casella" (L'Aquila) and in law from "La Sapienza" University (Rome). In 2006 he also graduated summa cum laude in electronic music under the guidance of Michelangelo Lupone. He has attended several specialization courses taught by Henri Pousseur, Sylvano Bussotti, Mauricio Kagel, James Dashow and Curtis Roads.

Walter Cianciusi has already released several pieces:
- "Miope" for electric guitars (Bèrben 2000)

Neil Horsky

An artist and resident of Jamaica Plain, MA., I conceive, realize and document event scores as an ongoing series entitled "Fluxusignments." I am very grateful to Cecil for including some of my childhood memories in this publication. Cecil is an inspiration to all contemporary Fluxus artists for his unquenchable creative spirit and devotion to the propagation of Fluxus. I trust that this collection of scores will inspire readers to harness their inner child, bringing joy to themselves and others through imaginative celebrations of life.

Mark Bloch

(b. 1956), also known as Pan, P.A.N., Panman, Panpost and the Post Art Network, is an American multi-media artist from Cleveland and Akron, Ohio, USA. He chose the vocation "avant garde artist" as a teenager when he heard of Yoko Ono. Later, exposure to Robert Wyatt, The Fugs and Frank Zappa convinced him this was a bad idea but it was too late. Bloch is a 1978 graduate of Kent State University where he was influenced by the performance artist Joan Jonas and videographer Taka Iimura, during respective artist-in-residencies. Bloch previously founded an offshoot of the local punk scene in Ohio called The New Irreverence and later participated with the "M'bwebwe" group in the their space on the Lower East Side of New York City in the early 80s.
Bloch is a self-publishing concept artist in the tradition of Dada, Surrealism, Marcel Duchamp, Fluxus, Ray Johnson, the New York Correspondence School, Situationism, "Pan-Neoism" and the DIY (do it yourself) movement. In his theoretical approach to issues of art and commerce, he refers to his activities as "Pan-Modern." He has occasionally called his work "Jung Fluxus" and "Fluxpan" as an homage to his frequent visits to the Emily Harvery Gallery beginning in the 1980s. In 2006, he was an artist-in-residence in Venice, Italy for the Emily Harvey Foundation.
His art uses the postal system as well as other communications media. Bloch created his first computer-related artwork in 1977. From 1989 to 1995, after over a decade working in mail art, he began to work on the Internet and created a "digital performance artwork in progress" called "Panscan" for Echo Communications. He now manages the www.panmodern.com website.
Bloch has done video, performance art, mail art and experimental music since the late 1970s and also works with networks, e-mail art, postcards, artistamps, rubber stamps, coded envelopes, and information theory, as well as comedy, journalism and broadcasting. He creates articles, pamphlets, books, and projects including his irregularly issued zine called Panmag (since 1980) and a cable TV show (since 1996) in New York called Panscan TV. The Cameron Museum of Art in Wilmington, North Carolina recently published "Robert Delford Brown: Meat, Maps, and Militant Metaphysics," which Bloch edited and designed.

Roger Stevens

Roger was born in 1948. He attended Coventry College of Art in 1968. There he became interested in Fluxus and produced many Fluxus pieces. From the mid-Seventies until the mid-Eighties he was very active in the Mail Art community as Roger Radio. Although he still produces art from time to time he now mainly writes and performs for children, plays in a band and makes films on You Tube. Type happy2oblige into the You Tube search engine to see some of his poems.

Keith A. Buchholz

A St. Louis area artist specializing in Intermedia and Fluxus. He grew up in southern Illinois, began showing work in the region in 1978, and held his first St. Louis show in 1983. Over the years, works have included large scale installation pieces, sculpture, documentation, Audio , Video, and Mail Art networking. He is a member of the International Union of Mail Artists , FLUXUS , International Fiber Collaborative , FLUXNEXUS , and FLUXUS / WEST , among other assorted organizations . He has shown work in over 40 countries in the past year, and was recently chosen as one of 30 American Artists to show their work in Kennedy Center, Washington D.C. as a voice for Global Warming. Keith currently operates Fluxus/St. Louis as a home base and studio, and an outpost connecting St. Louis to the world Fluxus network. He additionally collaborates on ongoing Fluxus projects worldwide.

Matt Taggart 1977-present

Growing up in rural Wyoming and Montana for most of his Life, Taggart has spawed an interesting perspective towards music and performance given the fact that both states don't have an established experimental scene of any sort. So direct influence was not an option. Ideas were realized by Taggart himself and later validated by finding out of other artists around the world thru reading books, magazines and the internet.

Taggart is and has been interested in pushing what music is and suppose to be through exploring improvisation within solo and group settings and recently within event scores and theater performance.

Taggart has released over thirty noise albums over the last six years and has performed all over the United States as pcrv aka pop culture rape victim. Recently Taggart has begun to explore electric bass within noise settings and also within event scores. Fluxus to Taggart is an extension of what he has been searching for within music and life.

Cecil Touchon

(Born 1956 - Austin, Texas) Touchon is a widely collected visual artist, poet, publisher and composer associated primarily with collage techniques. Founder of the Ontological Museum which includes Ontological Museum Publications, The Fluxmuseum, the Archives of the Eternal Network and the International Museum of Collage, Assemblage and Construction, Touchon has been working with Fluxus ideas since the mid 1970's. Touchon first become involved with the Fluxus community in 1998 via the Fluxlist.

Web: touchon.com

NOTES

---

[i] The following are two emails posted to Fluxlist related to the idea of canonization of Fluxus

Fluxus - Cecil Touchon Sun Sep 14, 2008 10:17 am

If you're a historian or collector then you want Fluxus to be dead as soon as possible. If you are a Fluxus artist you want it to live for ever. There it is in a nutshell.

The whole idea of it comes from the Catholic Church traditions of canonizing saints. They have to be dead before you can glorify them. But that does not mean that you should kill the saint in order to revere them. But if you have built a church to that saint that you hope to profit from and it cannot be opened until after their death, then the saint beware!

We are Fluxus and Fluxus is Ours – Cecil Touchon - Sun Sep 14, 2008 12:23 pm

What can we do about keeping Fluxus from being canonized as a collective?

The canonization of the individual artists who participated in Fluxus is one thing - fine and dandy, may it happen to us all! But Fluxus itself is impervious to canonization. We need to separate these two things from one another. I think one idea is to dismiss the idea that Fluxus is a historical entity and that the very idea of it is antithetical to Fluxus and preposterous and that anyone supporting such an idea knows nothing about Fluxus and has nothing to do with Fluxus. This needs to be done collectively by developing appropriate propaganda that is ubiquitous among us. We have to create a united facade through cooperative endeavors. We need to publish books which several of us are now doing of new work not history books about old work; leave that to the outsiders. We need to get articles in magazines. We need to establish a viable collector market for current work according to our own design. We need to validate ourselves through our own institutions. Thus the Fluxshop, Fluxmuseum, Fluxnexus, Fluxus Laboratories, Fluxlist, fluxlist Europe, Open Fluxus and so on. Then we need to gather as a group not to promote old but current and emerging Fluxus. Thus the Fluxus Brainstorm Gatherings. We need our own collective performance workbooks in order for us to promote each other's work as developing at fluxcase.com. We need to provide universities with materials so that upcoming students accept us as Fluxus and join our ranks. We need to demonstrate that we are Fluxus and Fluxus is ours. ...the first thing is establish lines of communication, the second thing: infrastructure. Third: practice, Fourth: product, Fifth: market, Sixth: endurance and sustainability. Theory and what not grow out of practice. Do it, then theorize about it.

I think of us as dervishes as in the Sufi tradition. If you ever ask a dervish if he is a Sufi master he always says no and promotes all the other dervishes that he knows as the masters. We should do the same: each one adulate the others, each one promote the others, each one honor and respect the others. This is how Fluxus will survive and deserve to survive: by our mutual good will toward our group and each other. We then are, through the codes we adhere to among ourselves, practicing sustainable peace and prosperity.

Ok, that's all for now.

Check out

- fluxmuseum.org,
- fluxcase.com
- fluxnexus.com

Indulge in Luxury at Fluxshop.net

World Peace
Is Imminent.
Do Your Part!
peaceplaza.org

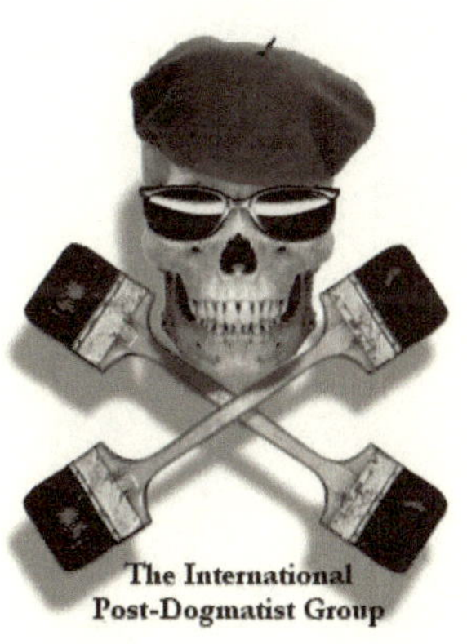

This book approved by
the International Post-Dogmatist Group
postdogmatist.com

www.ingramcontent.com/pod-product-compliance
Lightning Source LLC
LaVergne TN
LVHW091035080826
845145LV00002B/498

* 9 7 8 0 5 7 8 0 0 3 3 3 7 *